SPRING SHOOTS ON SUNFLOWER STREET

SUNFLOWER STREET
BOOK 1

RACHEL GRIFFITHS

COSY COTTAGE BOOKS

Copyright © 2020 by RACHEL A. GRIFFITHS

All rights reserved.

No part of this book may be reproduced in any form or by any electronic or mechanical means, including information storage and retrieval systems, without written permission from the author, except for the use of brief quotations in a book review.

❃ Created with Vellum

For my family, with love always

XXX

CONTENTS

SPRING SHOOTS ON SUNFLOWER STREET	vii
Chapter 1	1
Chapter 2	11
Chapter 3	20
Chapter 4	39
Chapter 5	57
Chapter 6	73
Chapter 7	88
Chapter 8	104
Chapter 9	117
Chapter 10	125
Dear Reader,	129
About the Author	131
Acknowledgments	133
Also by RACHEL GRIFFITHS	135

SPRING SHOOTS ON SUNFLOWER STREET

A little paint, a lot of hope, and the chance for a fresh start.

Lila Edwards never expected to be jilted on her wedding day. Now, she's content to stay hidden away in her cosy cottage with her two cats and her online craft business, avoiding the messy complications of love.

Ethan Morris has been drifting ever since his wife's death. Back on Sunflower Street to care for his mum, he's persuaded to start his own painting and decorating business. And when Lila's cottage needs a makeover, fate leads her to hire him.

As Ethan works to breathe new life into her home, the sparks between them are instant. But can they both move beyond their pasts—her broken heart, his grief—for a second chance at love?

1

'Lila! Lila Edwards, are you in there?'

Lila jumped as someone hammered on her front door. But it wasn't just someone, she knew full well who it was.

Roxie Walker: her best friend and fellow resident of Sunflower Street.

Lila dropped to her hands and knees on the floor behind the sofa, even though the curtains in her front room were closed and she knew there was no way Roxie could see through the heavy material.

'Lila! If you don't open this door in the next thirty seconds I'm calling the emergency services.'

Lila took a deep breath. It wasn't the first time Roxie had made that threat in the last few months, but it still caused a shiver to run down her spine. The thought of burly firefighters or police officers breaking down her front door and the fallout that would follow chilled her to the bone. All Lila wanted was peace and quiet, to fade into the background and be left alone to sleep, sing, cry and wallow in her memories. She certainly didn't want to be the centre of village gossip (yet again) and having a big red fire engine outside her cottage would set tongues wagging. This would be followed by donations of casseroles and cakes she'd never eat, and then there would be the exhausting task of trying to return the correct dishes and cake tins to the rightful owners while smiling and thanking them for the delicious offerings.

Just like last time ...

She wiped her eyes with the back of her hand, grabbed the arm of the sofa, hauled herself up to her feet then pushed her shoulders back. The big toe of her right foot popped through the hole in her fluffy red sock as if in protest, so she quickly removed the socks and flung them behind the sofa.

She could do this. She could open the door to her friend and smile, pretend that everything was just fine. Of course she could.

Lila shuffled out of the lounge and through the hallway, turned the key then opened the door, flinching as the light hurt her eyes. She tried to move her lips into a smile, but it felt far more like a grimace, and her top lip wavered. As she felt the full power of Roxie's gaze upon her, Lila's armpits tingled unpleasantly and beads of sweat popped out above her upper lip.

'Oh Lila…' Roxie shook her head, causing her jet-black hair to swish over her shoulders. Her bright green eyes, heavily lined with kohl, the lashes thick with mascara, were filled with concern. 'My poor, poor darling! How long have you been wearing it this time?'

As Roxie bustled into the hallway, bringing with her the vibrant aroma of tuberose and jasmine, Lila looked down at herself and stiffened. Roxie was right; Lila was wearing it again. But for how long? She really wasn't sure. She didn't even know what day it was.

She closed the door, shutting the world out, then turned to Roxie, but her friend was already speaking to someone on her mobile phone while opening the curtains. Lila watched as dust motes spun through the air, reminding her of tiny diamonds, making her wince as she recalled what she'd done with her engagement ring.

'Yes. That's right, Jo. Bride of bloody Dracula to be more precise. Looks like red wine but it could be sweet and sour sauce.' Roxie caught Lila watching her and mouthed *Sorry!* then returned to her phone call. 'Quick as you can, really, honey. And bring wine. Lots and lots of wine.'

∼

*E*than Morris flopped onto the single bed in his childhood bedroom. The room was like a time capsule and he could easily have been a teenager again, gazing at the posters on his walls of movies like Fight Club, The Matrix and American Pie and bands including the Red Hot Chili Peppers and Counting Crows.

He closed his eyes as exhaustion crept through him. He felt as if he could sleep for a month. In fact, that might not be a bad idea. He'd slept a lot in this bed over the years, especially when he was in his late teens. Back then, sleeping had seemed far more important than getting up early for school or college, although with his mother around, he'd often had his lie-ins disturbed as she had a tendency to vacuum the house every day before noon.

His poor mum. He'd come home to support her in her hour of need, or so he had told himself, but now that he was here, he was starting to realise that there was more to it. He wanted to be here too.

His mum hadn't been right for a while, but she'd kept it from him, only confessing that she had been feeling 'quite tired' and 'a bit run down' more recently. However, he'd managed to get her to admit that she'd felt this way for a few months and that she was starting to worry that there could be something more serious going on. His mother wasn't a hypochondriac, and rarely spoke about health complaints, so he knew there must be something wrong for her to admit to it. That filled Ethan with fear because she was all he had left, and the thought that she too was mortal was awful to contemplate.

Freda Morris was only sixty-three and had always been healthy and strong. She'd taken up running in her forties and Ethan had joined her, marvelling at how fit she was and at how she often outran him. In recent years, she had slowed down a bit and then a knee injury had stopped her running, but she still did yoga and Pilates at the village hall every week. She was slim, almost wiry, her grey hair was styled in a pixie cut that made her wise brown eyes seem huge and she easily looked a decade younger than she was. Freda was his mum: invincible and wonderful, and Ethan couldn't imagine the world without her.

But he knew all too well that people weren't immortal. That loved ones died. And that all the love in the world couldn't save someone if it was his or her time to go. The familiar pain stabbed his heart and he wrapped his arms around his chest and breathed slow and deep, focusing on his breath, waiting for the pain to ease.

~

*L*ila perched on a kitchen stool as her friends Roxie and Joanne fussed around her. She felt dazed, as if she'd woken from a nap in the sun, which was pretty much the way she'd felt on and off for months. Nothing had felt real for quite some time and she had the sensation of sleepwalking, that she never fully woke up properly each morning.

'Have you been eating, Lila?' Joanne rubbed Lila's arm. 'You're looking so pale and thin.'

'I eat.' Lila frowned, trying to remember what she last ate, then remembered it was half a bagel. But was that this morning or yesterday morning? Or even the day before?

'I don't think you do. That dress is hanging off you.' Roxie shook her head as she stirred something in a pan on the stove. Steam was rising into the air and Lila's mouth watered at the delicious aromas that drifted her way. 'This chicken noodle soup will be good for you, nice and nourishing.'

'You need a big bag of chips, Lila, and a cream cake.' Joanne pulled Lila into a hug and Lila's eyes burned with emotion as her friend squeezed her tight. Joanne was good at giving hugs, her soft curves and sweet floral scent always made Lila feel safe and cared about. But right now, Lila felt angular and awkward in Joanne's embrace.

'Noodle soup first.' Roxie carried the pan to the kitchen island and poured it into a bowl then gestured at the table.

'Let's get this into her before we do anything else. You can't think straight on an empty stomach, let alone give us your full Miss Havisham impression.'

'What?' Lila coughed as Joanne guided her to the table and pulled out a chair.

'You!' Roxie waved a wooden spoon at her. 'You're like Miss Havisham in that bloody wedding dress. All you need is the wedding cake and some cobwebs and you'd be all set to star in a Charles Dickens' novel.'

Lila looked from Roxie to Joanne then down at her ivory satin dress, noticing for the first time the red stains down the pearl-studded bodice and the grey hue of the hem that touched the floor. She hadn't meant to try it on again, but when she'd gone into the boxroom – where she kept the ironing board and basket, and a fair amount of junk – to put some clothes in the ironing basket, the dress was hanging there in its cover, the box with the beautiful ivory satin heels on the floor beneath it, and she'd been unable to resist. Problem was, once she'd managed to do up the tiny buttons on the back, almost dislocating her shoulder in the process, then added the veil to her lank blonde hair and stuffed her feet in their red socks into the shoes, she couldn't be bothered to take them all off again. Or was it more that she didn't want to take them off? She hadn't had her chance to wear the dress, shoes or accessories to her own wedding, so surely it was okay to try them on now and then?

'Lila?' Joanne had taken the chair to her left and Roxie took the one to her right. The chair opposite remained empty. *Four chairs.* It was meant to be the perfect family table, just as the cottage on Sunflower Street that she and Ben had purchased five years ago was meant to be the perfect family home. Lila had insisted on putting down a large deposit, using the majority of the inheritance her paternal grandmother had left her, which meant that their monthly mortgage payments had been very reasonable for such a lovely, character property. Lila had been naively smug back then, convinced that she was going to have the perfect wedding to the perfect man followed by the perfect honeymoon and the perfect life. Only it hadn't worked out that way because her perfect fiancé had run off with their perfect accountant on the morning of their perfect wedding. 'Oh honey... poor lovely Lila.' Joanne patted Lila's hand.

Roxie handed Lila a tissue. 'Let it all out, Lila, because it has to go somewhere.'

Lila nodded and surrendered to the pain, her tears dripping into her bowl of soup as her friends held her hands.

Lila might not have her own family, she might no longer have the love of the man she'd once thought of as her soulmate, but even through her pain, she knew that she had the very best of friends in these two women.

～

'That was delicious, Ethan, thank you.'

Freda smiled across the small square table at Ethan and he smiled back.

'It was nothing, Mum, just pasta bake.'

She shook her head. 'It's lovely having my dinner cooked for me. It doesn't happen often.' She met his eyes. 'Sorry, love, that wasn't a dig.'

'I know that, Mum, don't worry. However, now that I'm home I'll be doing a lot more to help out around the house.'

Freda reached across the table and took his hand. 'You're a good son. I was happy to see you head off into the world to live the life you wanted but I have to admit that I'm quite glad you're back for a bit. I've missed you.'

Ethan nodded. 'I've missed you too.'

Emotion rose in his throat, so he stood and picked up their plates then carried them to the sink. It wouldn't do to let his mum see him getting upset. What she needed right now was for him to be strong and take care of her. Freda was a good mum, had never put pressure on him for anything and when he was a child she had made him her priority, as if she was trying to show him how much she loved him in order to make up for his absent father. Ethan's father had left when he was a toddler. As a teenager with questions to ask, Ethan had tracked his father down, but the man he'd found and communicated with briefly via email had not been someone he wanted a relationship with, and it had seemed that his father felt the same. Living in Canada with a whole new family, his father did not want any links to his past. His emails were blunt and cold and although it had hurt Ethan initially, he had grown to believe that he was better off without his father in his life. However, Freda had done a damned good job without a partner around, and now Ethan wanted to repay her for all that she'd done by being there for her.

'I'll do those, Ethan.'

His mum touched his shoulder gently. He hadn't even heard her get up from the table.

'No you won't.' He shook his head. 'You go and sit in front of the TV and I'll bring you a cup of tea when I'm done here.'

'Ethan … there's no need to treat me like I'm on my last legs, you know.'

He turned and gazed into her warm brown eyes, so much like the ones he saw every day in the mirror, and smiled.

'I know that, Mum, and I know you're going to get better. I would like to spoil you a bit though, because I love you, and that's what people do for the ones they love.'

She paused for a moment then nodded. 'All right then, when you put it like that. I'll go and check what's on TV this evening, shall I?'

'Good plan.'

Ethan turned the tap on then filled the washing-up bowl. As he plunged his hands into the soapy water, he looked at his reflection in the kitchen window. It was dusk outside and bright in the kitchen, so he could see himself but still see the garden. It gave him an ethereal appearance, as if he were a ghost standing just outside the window, half there, half on another plane. And that was how he'd been feeling since he lost Tilly, as if he were half present, half absent.

Surely things had to get easier sometime soon? Or was he destined to exist in this limbo, never really feeling happy again? Never finding the old enjoyment in life that he'd once felt. Some days, he felt hope that he was healing and moving on, but others he could barely breathe with the pain and shock of it all.

He lowered his eyes to the bowl and started to wash up. One day at a time, the grief counsellor had told him. He was to be kind to himself, to *feel* his feelings and to observe them as they arose, to accept that he would hurt and he would miss Tilly and that it was perfectly natural. One day, the counsellor had promised him, his grief would ease and he would wake up without hurting.

One day…

2

The sound of birdsong filled the bedroom and Lila stirred, pulling the duvet up around her shoulders and snuggling back into the warmth. She had slept quite well last night and was pleasantly surprised because her nights were usually punctuated by toilet visits, tours of the cottage to check she'd locked all the doors and the occasional sobbing fit that made her nose stuffy and her eyes swollen, neither of which helped her to sleep well.

She gazed up at the white ceiling with its thick old wooden beams. It was exactly the kind of ceiling she'd imagined her dream home having and it added to the cottage's charm. Then her eyes moved across and landed on the large yellow-brown stain. High winds back in October had knocked a tile off the roof then heavy rain had leaked through. Lila had been forced to keep a bucket on the bed for two weeks until a local roofer had been able to replace the tile. The ceiling had since dried out but it needed painting. Lila hadn't been able to summon the energy to care. But now, in the morning light, it looked really bad.

And something smelled quite bad too.

What was that?

She rolled onto her side and saw her black and white rescue cat, William Shakespaw, sitting in the bedroom doorway, his slanted green eyes fixed on her face, his tail curled around his legs.

'Morning, Willy, how long have you been there?'

The cat gave a flick of his tail.

'What's up?' she asked, wondering why he was sitting so still, as if he was waiting for something to happen. 'Do you want me to get up and make your breakfast?'

Of course he did. He'd been out last night when Roxie and Joanne had been round, so he'd probably come home with the dawn, keen to eat then sleep. In the three years since Lila and Ben had adopted Willy and Cleocatra, Willy had always gone out at night. The cat flap in the back door meant that the cats could come and go as they pleased and Willy liked to spend his nights outdoors. Cleocatra, on the other hand, liked to spend her nights at home on the bed in the front bedroom, stretched out where it was warm and dry, which was where she probably was right now.

Lila threw back the top of the duvet and the smell grew stronger. She moved her foot and yelped. There was something in the bed and it was cold and sticky. The smell made her heave.

'William Shakespaw!' She only used his full name when she suspected he'd been up to mischief. 'What have you done?'

The cat stood up and slowly approached the bed, looking rather pleased with himself. Lila moved onto her knees and rolled the rest of the duvet back then let out a scream, because there, at the bottom of her bed, was a small, dead mouse.

'Oh, Willy, you don't have to do this you know. I appreciate the sentiments but you don't need to bring me... gifts.'

Gifts that he'd found, from the dreadful smell of decay, and not killed himself the previous night.

Willy meowed then jumped up onto the bed and sat next to Lila, waiting for her approval. She wanted to run to the shower and scrub her feet but she didn't want to hurt his feelings – daft as that may seem.

'I do love you, boy.' She smoothed his head and he began to purr. 'You really are kind bringing me gifts... even if this one is a bit... stinky.'

Willy pushed under her arm and climbed onto her lap. Lila stroked his soft fur and tried to breathe through her mouth. She'd have to wash the bedding, probably have to throw it out or burn it, and as she looked around her bedroom, she realised that she needed to do more than that. There were dirty clothes everywhere, the surfaces of the dressing table and chest of drawers had coatings of dust and the mirror of the wardrobe was hidden by her stained wedding dress that she'd left hanging there last night. For all she knew, Willy could have hidden twenty dead mice in her room and she wouldn't have been any the wiser.

'I've really let things go, haven't I, Willy?'

He rubbed his tiny head against her hand and his purring grew louder.

'Thank you for being here through it all.'

He gave her hand a little nip then, as if acknowledging her gratitude, and she pressed a kiss to his head. At least one of the males in her life had stayed and even kept bringing her presents. There was always something to be grateful for, you just had to know where to look.

Or, in this case, where to sniff …

~

*E*than stood on the doorstep of his mother's kitchen, gazing out at the garden. A few small birds chirped in the trees and somewhere in the village, a cockerel was greeting the morning.

The garden was starting to show signs of spring, the trees bearing small green buds, the snowdrops opening their pure white petals to the sun and the daffodils rising in the borders, their bright yellow a promise of warmer days to come. The fields that spread out behind Sunflower Street were also changing, as they did every year, and it was comforting to know that they always had and always would.

It had been strange waking in his old home, hearing sounds that were once so familiar and often ignored, like the creaking of the pipes under the floorboards as the heating kicked in and the clinking of glass bottles as milk was delivered from the local dairy farm. He had heard his mother rising twice in the night and held his breath as he waited to see if she was all right. Both times had been bathroom trips, confirmed by the flushing of the chain and the sound of the tap running.

Ethan had watched some inane TV with his mother last night as she dozed in her chair. He'd glanced at her from time to time, wanting to ensure that she was comfortable, that she didn't need anything, that she was still there. It had been like that with Tilly towards the end. He'd been by her side at the hospice, holding her hand as they stared at the TV in her room, trying to maintain some semblance of normality while knowing her days, hours, and minutes were numbered. The holistic care at the hospice had been wonderful and Ethan would be eternally grateful to them for how well they treated Tilly, but even so, it had been a dreadfully difficult time.

The pain surged inside him stealing his breath away as it always did. How could his sweet, lovely wife be gone? Tilly had been so full of life, so vivid and energetic, always laughing, always teasing, always so positive. It seemed truly unfair that someone who loved life so much should have it ripped away from her so cruelly and when she was just thirty-two. They had been trying for a family after deciding that it was a good time with Tilly established in her teaching role at a primary school, at the top of the pay scale but ready to start a family before she went after any promotions. Then one day, she'd been showering and she'd found the lump. From there it had been fast. Too fast.

She had gone from the GP to hospital where she'd been seen by a specialist nurse, had a scan then a biopsy. This had been followed by a discussion with a consultant, an operation, chemo, tests and more tests. But there had been bad news. More chemo. More bad news. Ethan pressed his fists into his eyes and ground his teeth together. It had all been so horrendously unfair and then… within a year, Tilly was gone, slipping away in his arms, a solitary tear running down her cheek and landing on her pyjama top.

Ethan turned and went inside. He sat down at the table and folded his hands in front of him, pressed one thumb down hard on the nail of the other one until the skin beneath it turned white. He had to feel this, had to go through it or he'd never heal. He knew that.

It was so tempting not to think about it, to push it all away and pretend that it had never happened. He'd done that sometimes back in Tonbridge in their old home, pretended that Tilly was still there, marking at the dining-room table while he made dinner. He'd pour two glasses of wine and take them through to the lounge, call her name and tell her to leave the schoolwork and come relax with him. He'd asked the counsellor if this made him mad and she'd smiled and told him to do what he needed to do for comfort. Some people had elaborate gravestones, went to church and prayed; some went to mediums and psychics and tried to speak to their loved ones; some kept everything at home exactly the same, keeping their partner's clothes and toiletries where they'd always been, unable to give them up because being able to smell them and to touch things their partner had touched helped them feel that their connection was still there. All of these things Ethan could understand and for him, for a while, on occasion, he pretended Tilly was still there in the next room.

Whatever helps ...

Eventually, with his mother being 'a bit under the weather', Ethan had come to the conclusion that moving was the answer. It had been time to sell the comfortable three-bedroom semi that Tilly had loved. The idea of leaving it had torn his heart in two, but living there without her for eighteen months plus the time she was in the hospice had been difficult. Her plants had withered, even though he'd watered them, the birds that had flocked to the garden to eat the seeds she put out for them daily had stopped visiting because Ethan forgot to fill the bird feeders, and the washing basket had seemed to overflow without Tilly and her obsession with emptying it (as soon as it contained so much as a pair of socks). It wasn't that Ethan couldn't do the washing, he most certainly could, but it had been one of the things that Tilly took charge of, just as Ethan washed the cars and filled them with fuel. Some of their mutual friends had joked that they were stuck in traditional roles, and in some ways he supposed they were, but then it was Ethan who cooked most of their meals and Tilly who did most of the driving if they went out in the car together. So Ethan had always let their friends' comments pass over his head while Tilly had laughed at them, confident that her marriage was exactly the way she wanted it to be.

After Tilly had gone, their mutual friends had been there for a while, offering meals and nights out and texting every evening, but as time had passed, they had moved on with their lives and Ethan had allowed their contact to wane. He liked them all, but they had lives to live, families to grow and their own problems to deal with, and without Tilly, it felt strange being around them; it was when he felt his loss even more. So, with his inability to commit to a job, having left his long-term one at a Tonbridge based building firm when Tilly was sick – because he didn't know how long he would need off – then spending just weeks with two different carpentry firms where he'd been unable to focus or to find the energy or commitment he knew he should offer to the jobs, there was nothing to keep him in Tonbridge anymore.

'Hello, love.'

Ethan jumped as his mother entered the kitchen.

'Hi, Mum.'

'You were up early.'

He nodded. 'Strange bed. Well… strangely familiar I guess. I've only slept in it a few times since I moved out.'

'Of course, because when you and T—' His mother's eyes widened.

'It's okay, Mum, you can say her name. I won't crumble, I promise.'

She inclined her head. 'When you and Tilly used to come to stay you'd have the back room. You could have that now, you know.'

He shook his head. 'I can't. I…'

'It's okay, Ethan, I understand. You need space from it all, from places you've been with her.'

'But please don't be afraid of speaking about her, Mum. Some days I feel like I'm going mad because no one else who knew her speaks about her in case they upset me. Not that I see many of them now.' He gave a wry laugh. 'I need to know that she did exist, that she was here even if for a short time. Tilly doesn't deserve to be forgotten. She needs to live on… at least in our memories.'

'Oh my darling boy.' His mum opened her arms and hugged him tight. His face pressed into the soft material of her dressing gown and she ran a hand over his hair. 'I am so sorry for your pain.'

Ethan tried to speak but his throat had tightened and nothing came out. Instead, he let himself be held, let his mother hug him like she'd done when he was a boy, and allowed himself to be comforted. He was a grown man, but right now he needed his mum, and he was okay with that.

3

'Black bags. Check! Bleach. Check! Rubber gloves. Check!'

Lila winced as Roxie went through their shopping list, loudly ticking each item off in turn. They were in the small village grocery shop and every time Roxie said something, all heads turned towards them.

'A bit louder, Roxie, I don't think the people in the next village heard you.' Lila shuddered with mortification.

Roxie paused and lowered her list then pushed her blue-rimmed glasses up onto her head.

'I'm just trying to make sure we don't forget anything.'

'I know, but… everyone can hear you and the way the list is going they'll think I haven't cleaned in a year.'

Roxie's dark eyebrows slowly rose up her forehead and heat filled Lila's cheeks.

'Okay, okay. So it has been about a year since I've... *deep cleaned*, I guess, but things have been difficult. I haven't had any energy.'

'I know that, Lila, honey.' Roxie shook her head making the bun of dark hair she'd pinned to the top of her head wobble. It was a style Lila had seen teenagers wear and she thought it looked as though they were off to ballet class, but Roxie liked to move with the times, as she put it, and her long black hair followed suit. With her amazing bone structure and clear skin though, Roxie looked good and Lila wished she had half her friend's elegance and style. Right now she felt frumpy and bland, as if she'd had all of her energy and zest for life sucked right out of her. She needed to get it back, to hop back on the life train, and hoped that a good spring clean would help her do exactly that. 'But finding that dead mouse in your bed yesterday has to be a sign that things need to... change.'

'It's not the first one Willy's brought home.'

'No, but perhaps he's trying to tell you something. The smell of the others could be lingering and making him think it's acceptable behaviour.'

'I have boiled the bedding you know. Actually, I put some of it in with the fabric recycling.'

'Glad to hear it. And please don't think anyone is criticising you here.'

'I know that no one is criticising me but it still seems awful, doesn't it? I've really let things go since Ben left.'

'Ben the basta—'

Lila covered Roxie's mouth quickly. 'Shhhh! Not here. You

can call him all the names you like in private but please don't swear about him in here.'

Roxie's eyes widened but she nodded so Lila removed her hand.

'Sorry about that but as angry as I've been with Ben, I don't think that slating him in public will do any good. There are still people here who probably blame me for him leaving and some who stay in contact with him, so I don't want them telling him that we still talk about him.'

'It hasn't even been a full year yet since he left you, quite literally, at the altar, Lila, so don't worry about what other people think. And who cares if he finds out that we're still sticking pins into a clay model of him and wishing that his willy would fall off.'

'Roxie!' In spite of her mortification, Lila giggled. 'We do not wish that his willy would fall off.'

'Just a bit of it?' Roxie gestured with her thumb and forefinger. 'About an inch.'

Lila shook her head.

'Or would that be all of it?' Roxie wiggled her eyebrows.

'You are incorrigible, Roxie.'

'I'm just trying to make you smile and it worked. If only for two seconds.' Roxie squeezed Lila's shoulder. 'I'm just still so mad at him for hurting you.'

'He'd stopped loving me, Roxie.'

'People do fall out of love, I know that, but he could have gone about things in a better way. Letting you arrange the wedding, letting you go to the church and wait for him then not showing. That was unforgiveable.'

'And yet all advice for healing a broken heart says that you have to forgive and let go. If not for the offending party, then for yourself.' Lila had read enough self-help books to know what she *should* be doing. Also, something Roxie had just said had struck a chord. *Letting you arrange the wedding...* When Lila thought about it, she had done all the organising, possibly even hurried it all along. Perhaps Ben's heart hadn't been in the idea at all and Lila had got carried away and in that case, blaming Ben – or at least placing the lion's share of the blame on him – was totally pointless. 'Anger and bitterness are heavy burdens to carry around.'

'True.' Roxie nodded. 'But with you, it's mostly been sadness hasn't it?'

Lila sighed. 'It has.'

The overwhelming, bone-weary sadness that penetrated every day, dulled the sunshine, sucked the joy out of everything and left her wanting to sleep each day away.

'But you're young and beautiful, inside and out. Joanne and I just want to see you happy.'

'How do I get there?' Lila asked the question she had considered hundreds of times since Ben left. 'How do I find happiness?'

'Well… there's no set formula. You need to heal from your pain, obviously. And you're doing that… although…' Roxie chewed her bottom lip.

'Although?' Lila questioned.

'Although I think you need to stop… wallowing now.' Roxie flinched.

'"Wallowing"?' Lila shouted then glanced around and gave the other shoppers an apologetic wave. 'I'm not "*wallowing*".'

'No, that was the wrong word.' Roxie grimaced. 'I didn't mean that you were doing this deliberately, or anything remotely along those lines, but what I do mean is that you're not going to feel any better while you're still dressing up in your wedding gown, veil and shoes (admittedly, sometimes with red socks) and belting out Whitney Houston hits until four in the morning. Aside from the fact that it's exhausting and leaves you drained all through the next day, it's not fair on the cats.'

Lila pictured Willy and Cleo, how he often disappeared all night and how Cleo headed upstairs. The poor loves used to sit on the sofa with her, snuggling up to her and purring contentedly. Now, they left the room when she put the karaoke channel on and set up the Bluetooth microphone. They'd never been Ben's cats but they must have missed him too, wondered where he'd gone and why he'd suddenly disappeared from their lives.

'You're right. I know you are. The dress though… it's like my only link to him and the love I thought we shared. I mean, after what I did with the engagement ring, the dress is all I have left.'

'I understand why you got rid of the ring, Lila.'

'It was a gut reaction when I got home from the church, but I do wish I hadn't flushed it down the toilet. I could have sold it.'

'You were entitled to react to being hurt and humiliated like that, Lila.'

'I do wonder if he ever loved me at all.' Lila swallowed hard.

'He did love you and probably still does in his own way, but he was and is a selfish pri—diot. He doesn't deserve you and one day he'll realise that he gave up the best girl in the world.'

'God, Roxie, I love you. You're so kind to me.' Lila grabbed Roxie's free hand and raised it to her lips. 'You just keep saying all the nice things and I'll try to stop wearing the dress.'

'There's only way we can ensure that happens.' Roxie cocked an eyebrow.

'Oh?'

'You need to burn it.'

'I can't burn it!' A horrid image of the beautiful dress that had cost over two thousand pounds going up in smoke made Lila's eyes sting. 'That would be terribly wasteful.'

'Incredibly cathartic more like!'

'No.' Lila shook her head. 'No burning it, but I'll… I'll do something good with it and I'll… donate it to charity.'

'Better get those stains out first then.'

'I will. Then I'll take it to the greyhound charity shop. That way, the dress will hopefully get its wedding and the money will benefit the dogs.'

'That sounds like a very positive step. I'm proud of you.' Roxie waved her list in the air. 'Now let's get the rest of these items then grab some baked goods from the café and head back to yours to begin Operation Bendgame.'

'Bendgame?'

'Yes. The end of Ben. Ben's endgame.'

'I'd prefer to call it something more positive… something that doesn't feature his name.'

'Okaaaay…' Roxie pouted. 'How about Operation… Spring Clean.'

'Not particularly original but definitely more positive.'

'Good! That's settled then and there's no better time to start than a Monday morning.'

'Indeed.'

'Next on the list is… candles.'

'Candles?'

'To make your cottage smell a bit sweeter.'

Lila cringed. 'Of course.'

And as they set off in search of candles, Lila pondered exactly how bad things had become in her lovely home. With the anniversary of Ben leaving fast approaching, it was a good time for a fresh start. She didn't want to move, certainly didn't want to leave Sunflower Street and her friends behind, so a good clear-out, deep clean and possibly even a few changes around the cottage would be a good alternative.

∼

'Is that you, Ethan?' his mother called from the lounge as he let himself into the hallway.

'Yes, it's me!' He smiled. Who else was she expecting?

He removed his trainers and set them on the stand beneath the coats then removed his running gloves and jacket. After a relaxing Sunday with his mother, he'd felt the need to get moving when he'd woken this morning and a run around the village had seemed like the answer.

Ethan liked to run. He enjoyed the way that it cleared his mind of everything other than keeping going forwards. He liked the noise of his trainers as they pounded the pavement and the sensation of the wind, and sometimes the rain, in his face. Running made his heart beat faster, his lungs work harder and his body come alive. He had always enjoyed running, but lapsed a bit as he'd settled into a comfortable routine with Tilly, but when she'd become ill, he'd taken it up again, knowing that he needed something to help him to de-stress, a way to work out his pain that didn't involve crying for hours on end. Crying had its place, but exercise was, for him, a more positive way of dealing with his emotions. Of course, he didn't always feel like running. Finding the energy and the motivation to put on his trainers and get out there when he yearned to hide under the duvet was a challenge some days, but he knew that he'd feel better for it afterwards, so he always made himself go.

He walked through the hallway and into the kitchen and found his mother sitting at the table, her glasses perched on her nose, the newspaper crossword open in front of her.

'The kettle's only just boiled if you want tea.'

'Water will be fine for now, thanks, Mum.'

Ethan filled a glass from the tap and drank it down in one go.

'Did you enjoy your run?' she asked.

'I did. It always helps.'

She nodded. 'I miss it. The sense of freedom it gives, the way it always focused me on what I was doing so I could let go of all my worries.'

'Sorry you can't go anymore.' Ethan sat opposite his mother.

'It's okay, love. I find that yoga is pretty good for taking my mind off things as I have to focus on my breathing. But I did love to run.'

'I would miss it too.'

'You should come to yoga with me now you're home.'

'What and stretch and bend with a load of women?'

'Men go too and the teacher is male. And it's a lot more than stretching and bending.'

He laughed. 'I know that, Mum, I just think I'd be too self-conscious. I mean… I can run but I'm not that flexible and I'd probably pop a kneecap or something.'

His mother smiled. 'No you wouldn't and you'd be surprised how quickly it improves your flexibility. It might also help you to relax. At least consider it.'

'I will. But only for you.'

'I'll hold you to that, Ethan.'

'I'm going to shower and dress then we can have a chat about plans for the week. What do you think?'

'I guess we do need to discuss some things now you're back.'

Ethan nodded. They needed to talk about what exactly was going on with his mother and her health as well as about what Ethan's role would be now he was home. He wanted to be here for his mother but he didn't want to get in her way either. He knew she'd hate to feel dependent on him.

'Before you hop in the shower, do you fancy going to the shop for some eggs? I can make you an omelette then.'

'One of your omelettes? How can I refuse?'

'Cheese?'

'Perfect.'

'Be quick then!'

Ethan gave a mock salute then went back to the hallway and slid his into his trainers. He was hot and sweaty but he wouldn't be long and he could shower when he got back. He grabbed his wallet from his jacket and left the house.

~

'I'm still not sure about this,' Lila stood outside the charity shop holding on tight to the black bag that contained her wedding dress. She gazed at the window display of a wooden greyhound sculpture surrounded by spring flowers made of crêpe paper and butterflies and birds made from silk. It was beautiful.

'It's time, Lila.' Roxie broke into her thoughts. 'You need to let go.'

'But… I could just put it in the attic, couldn't I? Out of sight, out of mind.'

Roxie shook her head. 'That won't work and you know it as well as I do. You'll find yourself climbing up there to get something else and before you know it, you'll be wearing the damned thing again. You have to go cold turkey.'

'Gah!' Lila shuddered. 'I know you're right. Okay. Let's go.'

Roxie pushed the door to the shop open then stood aside for Lila to enter. Lila shuffled inside with the bag and looked around. It was a lovely shop with warm and friendly staff, rows of colourful clothes, shoes and bags, shelves of books, games, CDs and DVDs and always had a seasonal window display specially designed to reflect the charity's good work.

They headed for the counter and waited while the shop assistant, a man with a shaved head and thick dark brows, who she guessed was around thirty, served an elderly lady who was purchasing a crocheted blanket made up of brightly coloured granny squares. When the lady had paid and walked away, Lila faltered. A hand in the small of her back pushed her forwards.

'Go on, Lila, you can do this,' Roxie whispered into her ear.

'What are you? My personal life coach or something?' Lila muttered, her belly now churning at the thought of what she was about to do.

'If you like.' Roxie kissed her cheek.

'Hello.' The shop assistant smiled, flashing fixed braces. 'Can I help you?'

'Yes. You can.' Lila cleared her throat. 'I have a donation.'

'That's wonderful.' He peered over the counter. 'What is it? The bag looks full.'

'It's my... it's a... it's my...' Lila's throat closed over and her eyes burned. This was the hardest thing she'd ever done. *Wasn't it?* Harder than sitting her driving test three times. Harder than hobbling around on crutches when she was sixteen after she broke her left leg ice skating. Harder than having to admit that Ben wasn't going to turn up for their wedding...

NO! It wasn't harder than that at all.

'I have a wedding dress that I'd like to donate. Along with a veil, shoes and other accessories.'

'A wedding dress, eh?' The man's eyebrows rose. 'We don't get many of those.'

'It hasn't been worn.' Lila realised that wasn't quite true. 'Well, it has. But not for a wedding. Or not *through* a wedding, anyway. See... uh...'

The man's blue eyes were filling with confusion and Lila's cheeks grew warm. What was she doing? She didn't need to tell him all this.

'What she means is that she bought the dress but didn't need it after all.' Roxie put an arm around Lila's shoulders and Lila sagged against her friend.

'Yes, that's what I meant.'

'Okay, well thank you very much. The houndies will be so grateful.'

'Houndies?' Lila asked.

'Greyhounds.' He smiled again. 'We call them houndies and I forget that not everyone knows that.' He pointed at the wall behind the counter where a large pinboard was covered in photos of greyhounds and smiling people. Lila had seen the photos on previous visits to the shop but never had a good look at them. She'd always been rushing around trying to get back for Ben, or to get something done for Ben, or to get something done before Ben got home. How had she lived like that for so long and not realised how much rushing around she did? 'These are some of our events, like the summer fête and some of the houndies that have been successfully rehomed. Every donation helps these gentle dogs, from rehabilitation after they leave the racetrack, to essential medical care, and to interim housing at the farm where they go before rehoming. Some of them are fostered for a while before meeting their forever families, but some of those end up being failed fosters.'

'What's a "failed foster"?' Roxie asked. 'It sounds very sad.'

'Not at all.' He laughed. 'I know *failed* is a deceiving word in this case. Basically, a failed foster is where someone fosters a dog with the intention of giving it up when a suitable forever home is found, but when it comes down to it, they find themselves unable to part with the houndie because they love him or her too much.'

'That's so sweet.' Lila sniffed.

'It is.' Roxie nodded at her side.

'We have a great success rate and it's all thanks to kind people like you.' His smile was warm and kind, and Lila smiled back. She actually felt okay about surrendering the dress and other items now because it was going to help such a worthy cause. She lifted the bag and set it on the counter, keeping hold of the tie handles.

'Thank you so much. I'll just take it through to the back then if I can take your details, I can put you on our system as a donor if you don't mind. It helps with Gift Aid which increases the value of your donation.'

'Of course.' Lila nodded.

As the shop assistant took hold of the bag, Lila's fingers remained tight around the handles and he stumbled as he tried to take the bag.

'Are you sure you want to donate this?'

Lila nodded.

'Lila you need to release the handles.' Roxie nudged her.

'I know,' she forced out through gritted teeth.

'Go on then.'

Lila slowly opened her hands, wiggled her fingers then pressed them to her chest as if afraid that they would grab the bag again. The shop assistant smiled at her then picked the bag up and hurried to the rear of the shop before disappearing into a back room. Lila's fingers itched to hold the bag again and her heart was pounding as if she'd run a mile, but she also felt different. Somehow lighter.

'You okay?' Roxie asked, her arm still around Lila's shoulders.

'I think so. I mean… I'm doing something good, aren't I?'

'You are and don't you forget it.'

By the time the shop assistant returned to them, Lila had composed herself and was ready to move on and leave her wedding garments behind.

Almost…

~

*E*than was walking home from the shop, carrying a box of eggs and a carton of milk, feeling quite upbeat about his morning. He reached the corner of the street and was about to cross when someone crashed into him, sending him staggering forwards and the box of eggs flying from his hand. He managed to keep hold of the milk and to right himself before he face-planted on the pavement but the eggs kept going and the crack as they hit the tarmac confirmed that they were broken.

He turned to see what had collided with him.

'No. I can't. I have to go back for it.'

A petite woman with blonde hair and a tear-streaked face was trying to get past a taller woman with long, black hair piled on her head.

'No, Lila, no. You've just done the right thing. A very, very good thing. Don't go back on it now.'

'But Roxie!' The woman called Lila stamped her foot in the way a frustrated toddler might do. 'I can't leave it there. It's my… my…'

'It's not yours now, honey. Come here.'

Roxie opened her arms and Lila stepped into her embrace. As Lila started to cry, Ethan was filled with concern.

'Excuse me.' He stepped forwards. 'Is everything okay?'

Roxie peered at him over Lila's shoulder.

'She's going through a bit of a life change.'

'Oh dear.' Ethan had no idea what that meant but it didn't sound good.

'Oh my goodness, did we bump into you just then? I knew we hit something but I was trying so hard to stop Lila going back to the charity shop.' Roxie frowned as she looked from Ethan to the egg box that was now leaking its contents onto the road, then back to Ethan. 'Were they your eggs?'

He nodded. 'It's okay, honestly. It was an accident.'

'I'll reimburse you for them. Just give me a minute and I'll dig my purse out.' Roxie pointed at Lila's shaking shoulders.

'No, it's fine. No need.' Ethan shook his head. 'I'll go back and get another box, but I'd better pick that one up first.'

'Hold on…' Roxie's eyes widened. 'You're Ethan Morris, aren't you?'

'Yes.' He nodded. 'And you're Roxie Walker. You live in the big house on Sunflower Street.'

'I am and I do. Gosh, I haven't seen you in years.'

'No. I lived in Tonbridge for about fifteen years and only came back now and then to see Mum, usually on flying visits fitted around my job and my wife's school holidays.'

'Ethan, this is Lila Edwards who also lives on Sunflower Street. Ethan is Freda Morris's son, Lila.'

The blonde head bobbed in acknowledgement and she softly said, 'Hello.'

'Hi, Lila, pleased to meet you. I'll just grab those eggs before a car runs over them,' Ethan said. He checked both ways for vehicles then stepped off the kerb and picked up the box, grimacing as sticky yolk ran over his palm. He looked around and spotted a bin, so he disposed of the box then dug in his pocket for a tissue.

When he returned to the women, Lila seemed calmer but her eyes were red and swollen and the tip of her nose was bright pink.

'I'm so sorry,' she said, meeting his eyes with her bright blue ones. Something in Ethan's chest squeezed as he gazed at her pretty face, her slender frame and her golden hair that seemed to shimmer in the February sunlight. Ethan had grown up in the village and had known most of the locals, but over the years, some had moved away and new people had arrived. A lot had changed and while he knew Roxie, but not very well, he'd never seen Lila. He would definitely have remembered her.

'Don't be sorry, there's no need. Accidents happen. Besides which, I forgot to pick up some cheese and if I go home without it, my mother won't be making my omelette.'

'Are you here to stay with your mother for a while?' Roxie asked then her expression changed. 'Oh my, I've just remembered… I'm so sorry. I heard about your wife.'

Ethan swallowed hard. 'Thank you. I've uh... I've come back to stay for a while. I sold my house in Tonbridge and my mother hasn't been well so I'm here to help out.'

'Good for you.' Roxie nodded. 'There aren't enough caring men around these days if you ask me. A loving son is a special find.'

Ethan wasn't sure what to say to that, so he lowered his eyes to his trainers, feeling quite selfconscious.

'Don't mind, Roxie.' Lila's voice was sweet as birdsong. 'She embarrasses everyone.'

'I do my best.' Roxie winked at Ethan. 'Right, as long as you're sure you don't want the money for your eggs, we'd better be going. Before Lila changes her mind again.'

'I won't change my mind. That wedding dress will make someone else very happy.'

Ethan's heart sank. So Lila was married.

'I donated my wedding dress, veil and shoes to the charity shop to help raise money for the greyhounds,' Lila explained. 'It was difficult to part with it. But I'm glad I have.'

'A wedding dress is very special to the person who wears it and that must have been hard to do,' Ethan agreed. 'But very generous of you. At least you have your memories and photographs of your wedding day.'

Lila's eyes widened and her mouth opened and closed a few times. She looked as though she'd seen a ghost and Ethan instantly wished he could take his words back. What had he said to upset her?

'Lila! It's fine. Don't worry now.' Roxie met Ethan's eyes. 'It was good to see you again, Ethan, and I expect we'll see you around.'

'I expect you will.' Ethan nodded, hoping that she was right and that he would see Lila again. Although, if she was married, as the wedding dress would suggest, then nothing would come of their meeting again. Not that he wanted anything to come of it, because he was mourning for Tilly and in no place emotionally to have a relationship or anything similar with anyone, probably ever again.

But as they said their goodbyes and he walked back to the grocery shop, he found himself wanting to see Lila again, to find out why his comment about her wedding day had upset her and why she seemed so sad. Such a lovely woman should never be sad or low. There should be someone doing everything in his or her power to make her happy. That was, in his opinion, part of being married; you should strive to make your partner's life as happy as possible because life was short and could be so difficult.

He wondered if his mother knew Lila, and determined to ask her as soon as he got home.

4

Lila walked into her bedroom and stood in front of the mirror. Her reflection stared back at her: petite, blonde, blue eyed, pale (almost grey) skin. It was like looking at a stranger, even though she saw her reflection every day. Surrendering the wedding dress yesterday had been challenging and she couldn't deny that she'd had nightmares about it, but waking up this morning knowing it was gone, had left her feeling freer than she had in sometime. When Lila had returned home with Roxie, they hadn't got much cleaning done but they had talked and laughed and Roxie had made Lila feel better, at least for a few hours.

Now, in her baggy grey jogging bottoms and faded blue T-shirt, Lila wasn't exactly dressed up, but even so, she could see how she'd let herself go. She had always made an effort with her appearance. Even after seven years with Ben, she'd wanted him to find her attractive and never wanted him to think she was becoming complacent. But it had been more than that, Lila had looked after herself for her too. She felt better if she exercised, cleansed and moisturised her skin, had her hair cut and coloured, ate well and drank lots of water. Her reflection was telling her that she hadn't done those things in a while, not consistently at least, and that made her chest ache. A broken heart could lead to self-neglect and Lila was guilty of that, but she understood why.

However, seeing the evidence in front of her like this would hopefully help motivate her to look after herself better.

Roxie appeared behind her then rested her chin on Lila's shoulder.

'Hey honey, what's up?'

Lila met Roxie's eyes in the mirror.

'The state of me.'

'You're beautiful, Lila. You always have been.'

'I've let myself go.'

'You haven't looked after yourself very well, but things will improve now. You'll see.'

Lila turned and hugged Roxie.

'You're such a good friend.'

'I love you, Lila. Besides which, you're my friend but also a kind of surrogate daughter.'

'You're not old enough to be my mum.'

Roxie laughed. 'I am just about, but I'd have been a teen mum. Okay then… surrogate sister.'

'You're like family.' Lila leant back and looked at Roxie who was wearing what seemed to be a navy boiler suit, white plimsolls and had a white and navy spotted scarf tied around her long hair. 'Better than family, in fact.'

'Lila, we are family. Haven't you heard that saying?'

'What saying?'

'Friends are the family we choose for ourselves.'

'That's beautiful.'

'I know. And it's true.'

'Shall we make a start in here?' Roxie asked as she released Lila and opened a black plastic bag.'

'I guess so.'

'Okay! So… What's going?'

'Oh…' Lila rested her hands on her hips and chewed at her bottom lip. 'Uhhhh…'

'Anything that's clutter can go. Some of it might be suitable for the charity shop, some of it can be recycled or upcycled. Some of it…' Roxie went over to the bedside cabinet that had been on Ben's side of the bed, seemed to notice something, crouched down then pulled something out from the narrow space underneath it. 'What the hell?'

She stood up holding something between thumb and forefinger, her face contorted by a grimace. Lila took the object from her then squealed and flung it across the room. It splatted against the wall then slowly slid down to the floor.

'Ugh!' Lila wiped her hand on her jogging bottoms.

'What was it?'

'Another of Willy's gifts I think.'

Roxie shuddered dramatically. 'Yuck! Yuck! Yuck! We need to wash our hands *immediately*.' She peered at the wall where a red-brown stain left by the small rodent resembled some kind of Rorschach test. 'And I need a coffee to calm down.'

'Good plan.' Lila nodded, glad of the excuse to delay decluttering her bedroom. At this rate, especially if they kept finding gifts from Willy, it would take weeks to sort out her cottage.

~

After purchasing more eggs, Ethan had gone home the previous day to shower and enjoy one of his mother's omelettes. They had eaten, drunk some coffee then his mother had gone to meet a friend, leaving Ethan to unpack some more of his belongings and to have some time to think.

He'd ended up hanging all of his clothes in the wardrobe and putting the rest into the chest of drawers then he'd realised that the windows were a bit grimy, so he'd gone out to the shed to get the ladder and a bucket, then cleaned all of them. When his mother had returned home later that afternoon, she'd been delighted to find shiny windows and that the bathroom floor no longer creaked – Ethan had lifted the lino and tightened the floorboards. There were a few more jobs around the house that he intended on getting done while he was home, and he'd found that he'd quite enjoyed the manual labour. It was nice to be occupied and to feel useful.

When he'd told his mother this over dinner last night, she'd made a suggestion that had set him thinking. It had been a very good suggestion and he was keen to consider it in more detail.

He'd been so caught up with eating and discussing his mother's idea that asking about Lila Edwards had completely slipped his mind, and it was only this morning when he woke that he realised he'd forgotten to ask about Lila. Still, it would keep and he had all the time in the world now to find out about the residents of Sunflower Street.

This morning his mother had gone off to yoga at the village hall. She'd tried to encourage him to join her but he wasn't quite ready for that, so he'd told her that he wanted to map out some ideas and fix the leaky tap in the downstairs cloakroom. The jobs he'd had in Tonbridge both before and after losing Tilly had equipped him with plenty of skills so he could pretty much turn his hand to anything around the home.

Sitting at the kitchen table, his laptop in front of him, he was researching his ideas and setting out some numbers. He certainly didn't need to worry about money, because Tilly's life insurance had left him well provided for, financially at least, but he also didn't want to let the next year drift by without feeling useful. He'd lost his direction when he'd lost Tilly and it was time to try to find it again. This might not be the right path for him, but he wouldn't know if he didn't try it and something about being back on Sunflower Street, spending time with his mother and bumping into Lila yesterday had lit a spark inside him that hadn't been there for a long time. He had been someone before he'd become a husband and then a widower, a person in his own right and while he'd loved being a husband then been devastated at being a widower, he wondered if he could find the Ethan he'd been before life had been turned upside down.

He intended on fanning the flames of the spark that had been lit to see where it might lead him.

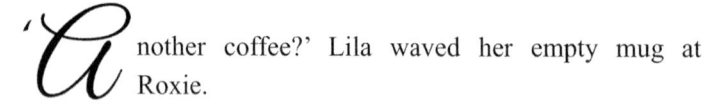

'Another coffee?' Lila waved her empty mug at Roxie.

Roxie pushed her sunglasses back on her head and frowned. They were sitting in Lila's back garden enjoying the late February sunshine. The sounds of birdsong, someone playing classical music on a piano further along Sunflower Street and the squeaking of a rusty swing floated through the air, soothingly familiar. The air smelt of soil, a deep rich aroma, as if the earth was preparing itself for spring.

Behind the garden, fields stretched out for as far as the eye could see, and Lila often gazed out from her bedroom window at the greenery beyond, watching cows grazing, lambs frolicking and tractors rumbling over the bumpy ground. Of course, having farmland right behind her home provided Willy with the perfect hunting ground, which was why he had access to so many small furry creatures but every area had some drawbacks.

'We've had three already, Lila, and it's becoming a bad case of procrastination now. We really should get cracking on your bedroom.'

'I know but it's so nice out here.'

'It's a little suntrap, your garden.' Roxie nodded. 'I could easily sit out here all day but we do need to get on.'

'Have you got plans tonight?' Lila asked.

Roxie's smile faltered.

'No… unfortunately. It'll be me and a good book, probably a bubble bath and a glass of wine.'

'Fletcher out again?'

Roxie inclined her head. 'Late business dinner, then he's staying in London.'

'Oh love, so sorry.'

Roxie shrugged. 'It's nothing new, is it?'

'No, but… it must be hard sometimes.'

Roxie adjusted the scarf on her head, released a deep sigh then nodded. 'It can be… hard, but I've had years to get used to it. I often think it would have been far worse if we'd had children because then they wouldn't have seen enough of him. However, I also wonder whether, if we'd had children, then he'd have been around more often. Would he have had a reason to come home every evening, a reason to spend time with us at weekends, a reason…' She fell silent and closed her eyes. 'Well, what can you do?' Roxie shook her head.

'Roxie? You okay?' Lila suddenly felt terrible for her friend. They rarely spoke about Roxie's marriage in this much detail because Roxie usually brushed it off, laughed it away with a wave of her hand, a joke and a glass of wine. Being busy, being strong, acting as though it didn't bother her was Roxie's way of coping with the fact that she did, clearly, miss her husband and wish that things between them had been different.

Lila had known Roxie for years and never seen this vulnerability before. Or had she just failed to notice it because until Ben left, her own life had been reasonably happy and she'd felt secure? What had changed for Roxie that had let the walls she'd built around herself slip? Was it seeing Lila's pain or was there something else going on?

'Is there anything I can do, Roxie?' Lila leant forwards and placed a hand over Roxie's.

'No, sweetie, I am absolutely fine. It's your life we need to sort out.'

'But you know I'm here for you too, right?'

Roxie nodded. 'I do. Now… let's get back inside and tidy up that bedroom. I do hope that Willy hasn't hidden any more… gifts.'

'Me too.' Lila wrinkled her nose. 'I'm horrified that he turned my bedroom into a rodent graveyard.'

Roxie stood up and held out a hand to Lila. 'Come on then, no time like the present.'

They went back into the cottage and Lila resigned herself to the task that lay ahead, but not before she'd vowed to find out more about what was going on with Roxie and her marriage. She would do anything she could to help her friend. Anything at all.

~

*E*than had decided to head to the village pub that evening to enjoy a beer and to look over his plans. He had his laptop, a folder under his arm and a spring in his step.

The latter was strange, to feel something akin to hope. It was an emotion that had eluded him for so long that he was very aware of it and almost afraid of it in case it was a trick. Was it possible that his mind could be fooling him and at any moment it would all come crashing down and the fathomless darkness would return?

He paused outside the door of The Plough and considered his thoughts. Of course it was possible that this was just a flash in the pan, a candle in the wind, a positive moment that would soon disappear. But it was good to have a positive moment, even if it vanished as quickly as it had come. Wasn't it a good sign that he was feeling some hope again?

It had to be a good thing.

He pushed open the door to the pub and entered the warmth that smelled of beer, chips and woodsmoke. He'd been inside so many times before and a host of memories washed over him, all linked to the familiar scents: coming here for a pint at seventeen, aware that the owner knew exactly how old he was and would never serve him while he was still underage, but asking for a pint anyway as it was a rite of passage. Bringing his mother here for birthdays and Mother's Day, for the pub quiz and with Tilly that first time he introduced them many years ago. He'd been so nervous that day, worried that his mother might not like Tilly and vice versa, but they'd hit it off immediately and he'd been able to relax as the two women he loved had chatted like old friends. He'd heard horror stories from male friends about animosity between their mothers and girlfriends, about jealousy and insecurity that could arise, about trying to maintain calm and being stuck in the middle until they were forced to choose between their mother and their partner. Then there were other tales about his friends' mother-in-laws and how they could never please them, how they'd always be struggling to prove they were good enough. Luckily for Ethan, his mother and Tilly got on.

As for Ethan's mother-in-law, Tilly's mother was sweet and kind, a practical woman who believed her daughter should make her own choices and be trusted to do so. It was why Tilly was such a strong and independent woman, Ethan felt sure. Her mother, Gwen, had instilled a sense of pride and ambition in Tilly that meant she would never *need* to be in a relationship, but would be able to choose to do so with a man she felt could be her friend, partner and equal. There had been times over the years when Ethan had found himself wishing that Tilly would seem to need him just a bit, or at least show him that she did, but he was full of admiration for her strength and independence, and even if she didn't show him much in the way of vulnerability, she did show him that he was loved.

He went to the bar and ordered a beer from a young man he didn't recognise, then took it over to a corner table close to the open fireplace where flames crackled and the warmth filled the air. It was a cosy, comforting space and some of the tension he usually carried around with him began to ebb away. He walked a daily tightrope of unease which meant that he was always conscious of when he was able to let go and relax.

Ethan placed his laptop, folder and beer on the table then removed his jacket and sat down. From here, he had a good view of the rest of the pub. There were a few people in, sitting at tables, enjoying an early evening drink and from the back room he could hear the sound of balls being hit with cues; someone was in there playing pool. He hadn't played pool in years. Admittedly, he'd never been very good, but he still enjoyed a game. Hopefully he'd have a chance to play again now that he was home.

Opening his laptop, he fired it up then double-clicked the document of his plans. As he ran his eyes over the words, Tilly came into his mind again. He hoped she'd be proud of him, trying to make something of his time here, trying to keep on living, even though it was difficult without her. He still saw Gwen every few weeks or so. It had been a few times a week a first, but as time had worn on, they'd seemed to drift apart, finding less and less to say to each other. All they had in common was Tilly; sometimes, talking about her was wonderful, but at others, it could be too painful. Ethan still sent Gwen regular texts, and she replied, but he suspected that their contact would continue to dwindle, especially now that he'd moved back to Wisteria Hollow. Gwen would never get over losing her only child, Ethan knew that, but she also needed to find a way to live with her loss. She was a busy woman, had her own PR business in Tonbridge, and Ethan suspected that her business would become even more of a focal point in her life.

Tilly's father, Nigel, was a businessman who travelled extensively with his job and spent a lot of time in Dubai. He and Gwen had separated when Tilly was a teenager but they'd maintained an amicable relationship for Tilly's sake. Ethan and Nigel had only ever had a polite and quite formal relationship, but Nigel had been a good father to Tilly. Nigel had spoken to Tilly on the phone or via Skype twice a week and made an effort to visit Tilly at least once a month, usually taking her out for expensive meals. Sometimes, Ethan went too, but he knew that Tilly liked to have time alone with her father, so he often made excuses not to go so she could have that precious time. Nigel had obviously been cut up about losing Tilly but since the funeral, he had spent more time abroad than ever and Ethan hadn't heard from him in over two months.

Ethan turned his attention to his plans and read them through then opened a design he'd created for his leaflets. It was basic but clear about what services he intended to provide and he'd double-checked it for spelling errors and ensured that it had all the important information like his contact details. It might not take off, this idea of his, but it might and it would certainly keep him busy if it did.

He closed the design, shutdown his laptop and sat back to enjoy his beer. Simple pleasures were to be savoured. This wasn't always easy to do, but he tried to remind himself of it every time the sadness threatened to consume him.

'Ethan?'

He looked across at the bar where a tall, slim man was waving at him trying to get his attention.

'Jamie?'

'It is indeed. Hold on!' The man turned back to the bar, paid for his drink then headed over to Ethan. 'I haven't seen you in bloody years, mate. How the devil are you?'

Ethan smiled at his old school friend. 'I'm not bad, thanks. Yourself?'

Jamie nodded. 'Good. Very good, in fact.' His expression changed suddenly, as if he'd been stung by a wasp. 'I, uh... I was so sorry to hear about...' He sighed. 'About your wife. Just... awfully sad.'

'Thanks.' Ethan met Jamie's hazel eyes and saw genuine sadness there. He'd been through this so many times in the past eighteen months when he bumped into people he hadn't seen in a while. It was always awkward, but better when people acknowledged it rather than pretending it hadn't happened or that they hadn't heard about it. Honesty and openness worked better for Ethan.

'I don't know how you cope. I mean…' Jamie blew out a long breath. 'It would break me.'

What could Ethan say to that? It had broken him. He was irreparably damaged, but how would that response help the situation?

'It's been the worst time of my life, Jamie, but I have to keep going. What's the alternative?'

Jamie inclined his head. 'Of course you do, mate. Of course you do. It must take the strength of ten elephants though… to get up and live every day.'

Ethan smiled. Jamie wasn't shying away from this, glossing over it or minimising it. He was trying to understand, trying to properly empathise and Ethan appreciated his efforts.

'Twenty elephants.' Ethan raised an eyebrow. 'Some days, thirty.'

Jamie smiled. 'So is it okay to ask how you're managing?'

'I just… do my best. Some days are darker than others.'

'Are you around for long?' Jamie asked.

'Not sure yet. Mum's been a bit under the weather and I decided the time was right to sell up in Tonbridge. It didn't feel right rattling around in a family home when it's just me.'

'I can imagine.' Jamie nodded. 'Did you have any children?'

'No. Sadly. But then, not so sad because if we had, they'd have lost their mum. So in way, it's a good thing I guess.'

'I'm sorry about that too.'

'Don't be. Not your fault.' Ethan gave a wry laugh. 'Look, Jamie, I'm really grateful for your understanding but please don't feel awkward. Everyone feels awkward when they find out I'm a widower and in all honesty, I just want to be treated like me. To *be* me again, even if just for a conversation.'

'Of course. Sorry again.' Jamie winced then ran a hand back through his thick ginger hair. 'It's hard to stop apologising.'

'Tell me how things are with you. Wife? Kids?'

'Yes to both. Well, actually, Donna is pregnant with our first. We've been in London for the past four years, living in a flat, but when she found out she was pregnant, we knew the time had come to seriously consider our options. I mean… living in a one bed flat with a baby just wasn't going to be practical. Plus, we both work full time and would have had to pay through the roof for childcare, so we made the decision to move back here and be near my parents. That way life will be a bit cheaper and we get family support.'

'Wise move.'

'We think so. I just hope Mum and Dad don't become too involved and stifle us both. Donna's quite independent and it will drive her mad if she doesn't get enough space.'

'I'm sure it will work out. Your parents were always very kind and welcoming.'

'Yes that's right!' Jamie laughed. 'All those times when I

used to have the entire football team round and Mum used to feed you all. I don't know why she put up with that.'

'My mum wouldn't have.' Ethan's mother had always been kind to his friends and didn't mind having one or two over at a time for dinner or a sleepover, but she drew the line at the full football team.

'I don't blame her. I can't see Donna or me wanting that when our little one is older.'

'Congratulations, anyway.' Ethan raised his beer. 'To you, Donna and your family.'

'Thanks, mate.' They clinked beers then drank. 'So I'll be seeing you around?'

'Yes. I wanted to be here to help Mum out and I hoped a change of scenery would be good for me.'

'Growing up, I thought this village was too quiet and rather dull but now I'm back here, as an adult and father-to-be, I see it differently.' Jamie frowned. 'Funny how perspectives change.'

'It's a lovely village and Sunflower Street looks pretty good to me too. It's comforting being back.'

'You working here this evening?' Jamie nodded at Ethan's laptop.

'I was.'

'Own business?'

'A new venture. I'm setting up my own painting and decorating business. Something to keep me out of mischief.'

'Good idea, Ethan. There's always call for handymen.'

'That's what I'm hoping.'

'You'll have all the old ladies ringing your hotline.' Jamie laughed. 'You'll be Mr Popular round here in no time at all.'

'I hope so!'

'Well, look, it's been really good seeing you.' Jamie drained his glass. 'We've got a busy few weeks ahead of us with moving and all that, but once we're settled back in the village, hopefully we can do this again?'

'I'd like that.'

'Brilliant.' Jamie stood up. 'Best get back. I told Donna I wouldn't be long and she gets a bit… crotchety if I don't stick to my word. The hormones are driving her crazy and one minute she's furious, the next she's sobbing. It's a minefield. She wanted me to go out for a bit so she could have a soak in the bath but if I'm gone too long, she'll start to worry. I told her it's different here and that we're not in the heart of the City anymore but she still gets anxious.'

'That's understandable.'

'See you soon, then.' Jamie shook Ethan's hand with the vigour of an old friend then he took his glass to the bar and left the pub.

Ethan finished his own drink. If only he had someone waiting at home for him. His mum would be there, but to have a partner, someone who loved him and wanted to spend time with him would be wonderful. The ache of missing Tilly, of missing being part of a couple opened again in his chest, the wound still too raw to completely heal. Finding a connection with another person was special and he wondered if he'd ever feel that kind of security and joy again.

It had been good seeing Jamie with his messy ginger hair, kind hazel eyes and the freckles that covered his nose and cheeks. He didn't look that different to how he had when he was a teenager, he'd just grown taller and filled out across the shoulders a bit. Ethan hadn't seen him in years but it was as if it had been just weeks. Jamie was still easy to talk to, still funny and friendly, and Ethan hoped he'd see him again soon. Many people found it difficult to be around Ethan, feeling the subject of his grief too overwhelming to navigate, some of them seeming to fear that it might be infectious and that they too might lose someone they loved. Ethan could understand that and he'd let people leave his life without putting up a fight for them, watched some of his mates and Tilly's back in Tonbridge disappear from his life, accepting how difficult it was for them. He'd have found it difficult too, he knew that. But Jamie had been open and honest and Ethan appreciated that.

His thoughts drifted towards Lila and what his mother had told him about her earlier that afternoon when he'd found a chance to ask her. Lila had lived in the village for a few years and bought a cottage on Sunflower Street with her partner, Ben. They'd seemed happy enough, his mother had said, although she admitted that she had felt that something was off with Ben. It was, in his mother's words, 'a gut feeling' that Ben wasn't an honest character. His mother had said that Lila and Ben were both busy, he left for work early and returned home late and therefore she saw more of Lila than of Ben. However, she said she hadn't got to know Lila very well as the younger woman seemed to spend a lot of time rushing around, even though she ran her own business from home. They sometimes crossed paths in the village wool shop and exchanged pleasantries, then Lila would go rushing off again.

Lila and Ben had been about to get married, in a small ceremony of close friends and family – his mother knew this because a neighbour had told her – but Ben had failed to show up at the church. He had jilted Lila at the altar. It was a terribly sad affair and Ethan's mother expressed her sympathy for Lila, having been abandoned by her own partner many years ago. She had taken Lila a few meals in the following weeks, but that had been about a year ago, and life on Sunflower Street and in the village had moved on. As it always had done and always would. Sad things happened but people survived. Lila was a survivor just like Ethan.

Time now to go home and rest, to think and to plan. Jamie seemed to think Ethan's business was a good idea. Ethan hoped he was right.

5

Lila placed her mug on the draining board then wiped her wet hands on a towel. She turned and looked around her kitchen, at the dresser that was now tidy and dust free, at the slate floor that had been swept and mopped, at the large fridge with its magnets with quotes about friendship and seizing the day, with sweet motivational phrases like *Life isn't about waiting for the storm to pass, it's about learning to dance in the rain.*

She sighed as she let the words sink in. There had certainly been storms in her life and she did love to dance, but could there be dancing in the rain? Was it possible to smile even when times were tough? Lila really hoped so. She also hoped that the storm would eventually pass and leave behind a calm, sunny day.

Strolling around her cottage, she admired how clean and tidy everything was. Roxie had certainly made an impact on her home and helped her to get rid of anything she didn't need, especially things that reminded her of Ben and would be of no help with her recovery; also known as moving on.

But something was missing today. The sunshine was streaming in through the sparkling windows, the floors were warm, the aromas of furniture polish and vanilla candles filled the air and she felt better knowing that there were no dead rodents stashed under her bed, but even so, the cottage was so quiet. It would be this quiet all day and all night unless she filled it with noise, with music and song. Her nights of singing had done this for her as she'd danced and sung in her wedding gown, trying to banish the silence, the loneliness, the emptiness. This cottage had been meant to house a family, to hold Lila, Ben and their babies safe within its walls, to watch over them as they grew, to show physical signs of this as Lila and Ben drew on the doorframe to show how their children were getting taller. Lila had imagined it all over the years. She had envisioned babies being brought through the front door in a brand new car seat, nursed in a fancy rocking chair upstairs. She had pictured holding chubby hands as little ones toddled around the kitchen and garden, supervised them as they baked cookies and muffins. Her heart had soared at the thought of celebrating birthdays at the kitchen table, cheering as her children blew out the candles on their cakes. It had all seemed possible, seemed real, seemed to be the perfect dream.

Then Ben had blown it all apart in an instant.

But now Lila knew that what she'd thought she and Ben had, had never been real, it had been a dream, and like most dreams it had held little substance. And now it was long gone. Like Ben.

What she was missing most today was Roxie. Her friend was so full of life, of enthusiasm and joie de vivre that she filled a room, made a house into a home, pushed the shadows away.

Having her company had helped Lila and she wished Roxie could have stayed on. But Roxie had her own home and life, of course, including some issues with her marriage that she needed to deal with. Lila knew that nothing was perfect, that all relationships had difficult times, and she hoped with all her heart that Roxie and her husband would work through theirs. Roxie deserved to be happy.

As did Lila.

She knew that.

It didn't help though when she was trying to pull herself together enough to actually get some work done.

Work. Yes. It had to be done and soon.

Wallowing like this served no one. Her little business that she'd treated like a baby for some time was floundering and neglected. She had money to live on, including some of her inheritance that was in a high interest ISA, and Ben had signed his share of the cottage over to her because she'd paid the deposit and, Lila suspected, because he felt guilty. She had offered to buy him out but instead he'd taken the money from their joint savings account, a considerable sum, and Lila hadn't pushed him to take more. She'd been angry and hurt and it had made her more ruthless than she'd have been otherwise. She suspected that Ben had been surprised, and might even have expected her to try to persuade him to take more, but she hadn't, and so he'd walked away financially worse off than he could have been.

Lila also had some money that Ben had no idea about, that she'd squirrelled away for when she became a mum, and though she hated the thought of spending that, she would do so if her situation became desperate. However, it would be better if she could start earning again, rebuild her business and have a reason to get up in the mornings.

In the lounge, she sat on the sofa and her eyes fell on her crochet basket. She'd loved to crochet and had made lots of lovely gifts for friends in the past and some for herself, from cute animals to Christmas tree ornaments, and toys for the cats. What if she opened the basket and took a look inside? Just to see what was in there, of course. No pressure. No strain. Just a look.

She leant forwards and pulled the basket closer then opened the lid. As she lifted out the pink leather purse that contained her crochet hooks, a flicker of excitement stirred inside her and a flame was lit. She could crochet some animals. But what first? What would people want to buy?

An image filled her mind and her lips curved upwards.

Yes, of course. That would be just perfect.

∼

'What's with all the secrecy?' Roxie asked as Lila led her through to the kitchen, holding a hand over Roxie's eyes.

'I have a surprise for you and I want you to see it all in one go.'

'Okay…' Roxie's eyelids fluttered as Lila withdrew her hand.

'Ready?'

'Ready!'

'Open your eyes!'

Roxie blinked then gasped.

'Oh my goodness, Lila! You have been busy.'

Lila nodded, pride filling her as Roxie hurried over to the kitchen table to take a closer look.

'You did all this in a week?' Roxie asked.

'I did. After you'd gone, it was dreadfully quiet here the next day and I started thinking about what I could make to keep busy.'

'Greyhounds seemed like the right choice?' Roxie nodded.

'Yes. Going to the charity shop inspired me to make some. I created my own pattern then made them in lots of different colours.'

'I've got to admit I've never seen a pink greyhound or a blue one before.' Roxie picked up one of the crocheted toys and moved its long legs back and forth, a big smile on her face. 'They're just gorgeous, Lila. You're so clever.'

'Thank you.' Lila released a breath of relief. She'd made twenty of the wool dogs since last week, using up all the different colours of wool she had in her basket and topping up with a few balls from the local wool shop. As each one was finished, she added it to the pack on the kitchen table and soon she could clearly see the fruits of her labours. After the first three, she'd known the pattern off by heart and had been able to crochet as she watched TV or listened to the radio. It passed the time and kept her occupied. It had also inspired her to create other animals to sell online and she thought she'd be able to make them to order too. She intended on donating some of the greyhounds to the charity shop, hoping that they would raise money to help the rescue dogs. After all, they had been her inspiration.

'What time is Joanne coming over?' Roxie sat a greyhound up on the table with its legs splayed so it wouldn't fall over.

'She should be here soon then we can eat.'

'What are you cooking? It smells delicious.' Roxie made a show of sniffing the air and approached the Aga.

'Salmon and asparagus quiche.'

'Ooh!' Roxie clapped her hands. 'That does sound wonderful. Anything I can do?'

'There's wine in the fridge so you can open that if you don't mind and I'll put a salad together.'

'Sounds like a great plan.' Roxie went to the fridge and located the wine while Lila washed the salad leaves under the tap then set them to drain, all the time her heart fluttering with happiness at Roxie's reaction to the crocheted greyhounds.

~

*E*than felt like he was fifteen again, doing his paper round as he walked around the village delivering leaflets. He'd already been stopped three times by elderly locals keen to grab him for a conversation and one old lady had recognised him as Freda's son and insisted he go in for a cup of tea and a slice of cake. He'd stayed for over an hour, realising that the lady was lonely and enjoying having company. When she'd started to lead him around her home, showing him possible jobs that needed doing, he realised he could end up working there for months. He'd eventually left her when the familiar music of a well-known TV soap started and she rushed to her chair to watch the drama unfold, but not before she'd pressed a foil-wrapped slice of cake in his hand and made him promise to come back soon.

The air had grown cold as he'd walked the streets, posting his colourful leaflets through doors, thinking of the stew his mother was making for tea. He was looking forward to eating it and spending the evening with his mother. It was funny how simple things like that could be so enjoyable when you reached your thirties, because as a younger man, he'd have laughed at the idea of an evening at home being something to anticipate. Now he was glad of the company and home comforts.

When he'd completed his delivery around the village, he turned back to walk home, already dreaming of the warmth he'd find there in terms of food and love. He just needed to post the last of the leaflets on Sunflower Street and then he'd be home.

∽

*L*ila was sitting at the table with Joanne and Roxie. They all had goblets of wine and full plates.

'Cheers my dears!' Roxie held up her glass. 'To friends like us.'

'Cheers.'

They all clinked glasses then drank.

'This wine is delicious, Lila.' Joanne picked up the bottle. 'Where did you get it?'

'It's from the local vineyard.' Lila smiled. 'I popped into their shop last week and bought a few bottles.'

'Really?' Joanne frowned. 'I know that new owners took over last year but I thought they only stocked wine at supermarkets. I didn't realise they had their own shop.'

'I saw the sign when I was driving past so thought I'd take a look. Perhaps they realised that selling locally could be a good thing too.' Lila sipped her wine. It really was delicious, floral and fruity, not too sweet or too dry.

'I love what you two have done round here.' Joanne gestured at the kitchen. 'Everything is much tidier.' Her cheeks coloured. 'Oh goodness, Lila, I'm sorry. That sounded awful. What I meant was that I'm glad you've been able to… find more space.'

Lila giggled. 'I know what you mean and it's fine. I'd sunk into slobbery as my grief dragged me down, but having a good clear out was very cathartic and I'm so grateful to Roxie for helping me.'

'I would have helped too, Lila, but I've had so many shifts at the café because I'm trying to save and—'

Lila held up a hand. 'Joanne, I didn't expect you to help. I know how busy you are. I didn't actually ask Roxie to help but she volunteered.'

Roxie laughed. 'I twisted your arm behind your back and forced you to do it, you mean. It was just time to sort things out, honey. You'd hit rock bottom so the only way was up. Besides which, I had the time to help you out.'

Lila nodded and looked down at her plate. The quiche was scrumptious with its light, golden pastry and perfect combination of salmon, cheese and asparagus. She'd served it with potato salad, juicy red tomatoes and dark green spinach with basil olive oil sprinkled over the leaves.

'What's next?' Joanne asked. 'Are you going to make more greyhounds?' She nodded at the dresser behind them where Lila had piled all the crocheted dogs to clear space on the table.

'Yes and other animals. I'll get them photographed and listed in my online shop then see if I get any commissions too.'

'They are adorable.' Joanne smiled. 'We might be able to sell some at the café.'

'That would be great, thank you. I also think I need to get some work done here.' Lila peered around her kitchen. It was warm and cosy but now that everything was tidy, she could see what needed to be done. The window that overlooked the garden was loose and rattled in its frame on windy days. Lila had become accustomed to the noise, but knew that it needed sorting. She could get a whole new window or see if someone could redo the seals. Then there was the cupboard under the sink where the door had come off its hinges. She rested it against the cupboard frame but it wasn't a long-term solution and sometimes she forgot and pulled it open only to have it land on her toes. Upstairs, there was the stain on her bedroom ceiling and all of the walls could do with painting. 'There are things I can't ignore any longer plus I think a coat of paint would freshen everything up.'

'You could do the painting yourself,' Roxie suggested. 'I could help with that.'

'I'm not letting you do another thing round here, Roxie. You have your own life to lead too. But thank you, anyway. Yes, I could paint but it would take weeks and if I get someone in to do it then I can focus on being creative and hopefully start to earn some money.'

'I think that's a very good idea.' Joanne nodded. 'To creativity!'

They all drank some more wine.

'Was that the door?' Roxie asked, looking up from her glass.

'I think I heard the letterbox go but it could have been the wind.' Lila stood up. 'I'll go and check.'

She headed through to the hallway and saw something sticking through the letterbox. She pulled it through, read it, then smiled.

Back in the kitchen, she held it out to her friends.

'Look at this! Talk about fate.'

'What is it?' Roxie peered at it. 'I haven't got my glasses on. Read it to me.'

'It's a leaflet for a local painter and decorator. It says "*No job too big or too small. Reasonable quotes. Friendly and reliable*"... "*experienced*" ... and so on.'

'Is there a name on it?' Joanne took the leaflet from Lila. 'Yes! It says "*Ethan Morris*" and there's a number.'

Roxie frowned. 'Freda Morris's son! Well how about that?' She flung up her hands. 'Isn't it handy that he moved back to the village?'

'Handy!' Joanne laughed. 'Because he's a handyman.'

Roxie and Lila shook their heads.

'Roxie, I meant to ask you after we bumped into Ethan that day and destroyed his eggs… what did you mean about his wife? You said you were sorry about her.'

Roxie nodded. 'I did. Don't you remember about eighteen months ago, Freda lost her daughter-in-law?'

Lila frowned. Now that Roxie mentioned it, she did recall something about Freda losing a family member but she hadn't really thought any more about it because the relative hadn't lived in Wisteria Hollow so the funeral hadn't been local.

'How did it happen?' Lila asked Roxie.

'Cancer. Apparently it happened very quickly and she was very young.'

'How tragic.' Lila rubbed her chest, sympathy for the poor young woman, Ethan and for Freda flooding through her. 'We never know what other people are going through do we?'

'We don't.' Roxie shook her head. 'However… back to you and your current issues… You need to phone Ethan right now and book him. If he's posted these around the village there'll be loads of people after his services.'

'I'm sure it can wait until tomorrow,' Lila said, her stomach now churning.

'No it can't. You need work done and he's available. It's fate. So secure his time now while you can.'

'But I don't like to put on a man who's lost his wife and been through so much.'

'Lila, this is his business and seeing as how it's new to the area, he'll want to get it off the ground. Therefore, rather than hindering him, you'll be helping him. Think about it that way.'

Lila looked at Roxie then at Joanne and both of them nodded. They were right. If Ethan got booked up it could take months to get him here and if he was starting over in the village then this would be a positive thing for him too.

She grabbed her mobile off the dresser and started to type.

'What are you doing?' Roxie frowned.

'Texting him.'

'"Texting"?' Roxie grimaced.

'Yes. It's fine, I'm sure. He's probably having his dinner now and I don't want to disturb him. If I text, he can reply when he's ready.'

Lila pressed *SEND*.

'She's right.' Joanne looked at Roxie.

Half an hour later, they were tucking in to raspberries, meringues and clotted cream when Lila's mobile buzzed. She jumped and looked up. Roxie and Joanne were grinning.

'Go on then, see if it's him.' Roxie picked up Lila's mobile off the table and handed it to her.

Lila looked at the screen then swiped her thumb across it.

'It's him. He said… He can come round tomorrow and take a look.'

Lila's stomach did a somersault and she took a sip of wine to wash down the meringue that seemed to have lodged in her throat. Why was she anxious? Why such a visceral reaction to a text message?

'Woo hoo! Fan-bloody-tastic!' Roxie clapped her hands. 'Time to celebrate with another bottle of wine.'

While Roxie got up and went to the fridge, Lila replied to the text, suggesting Ethan come round at ten. That would give her time to do a quick look around to ensure Willy hadn't brought anything in overnight and to prepare to have a man in her home. There hadn't been a man past her front door since Ben left and that had been fine with Lila, so the thought of having a man in here was somewhat daunting. But, of course, he was a workman coming to look at a job and that was all.

Lila could cope with that. It was another positive step in her journey to rebuild her life. She owed it to herself and her friends to see it through.

∽

Ethan stood outside Lila Edwards's front door and took a deep breath. It was silly to be nervous, he knew that, but this was his first opportunity to give a quote on some work and it had come through so quickly. He hadn't expected to be asked for a few days at least, but after delivering the leaflets last night, Lila had sent him a text almost immediately. Perhaps he had been right to decide to try this venture; perhaps it was a positive step that would reward his efforts.

He knocked on the door and waited, taking the time to look over the front of the pretty cottage. It was double fronted with latticed windows set back in thick stone walls and had a tall, thick chimney on the roof. Ivy climbed the front of the cottage and there were planters underneath the ground-floor windows where rose bushes sat, dark and bare, their beautiful fragrant potential being stored for warmer days. In the summer, the cottage would look chocolate-box perfect with climbing roses and likely smell just as good too.

The door opened and Ethan smiled at the pretty woman who stood before him. With her blonde bobbed hair, blue eyes and pale skin, she was breathtaking and his heart sped up.

'Ethan?' she asked.

'Yes.' He nodded. 'Hello again, Lila.'

'Come in, please.' She stepped back and he followed her into a cool, dark hallway that smelt of woodsmoke, vanilla and some citrus scent that could be lemons or limes, possibly bergamot. 'We can go through to the lounge.'

Lila showed him into a cosy room with a low ceiling complete with dark wooden beams and two fat red sofas with patchwork blankets draped over their backs. There was a coffee table covered with what looked like knitting, a log burner and wooden mantelpiece, and a small TV set in the corner. It was a room that looked lived in. He scanned for photos but apart from one of Lila with two other women, one of whom he recognised as Roxie from the other day, there weren't any others. It seemed unusual not to see family photos or romantic couple ones. But then, if Lila had been jilted on her wedding day, it was hardly surprising.

'I know, it needs to be freshened up.' Lila sat on one of the sofas so he took the other one.

'I was just admiring the place. It's lovely. Really cosy,' he said truthfully.

'It's home, I guess.' She shrugged. 'Sorry I didn't ask, would you like a cup of tea or coffee?'

'No, thanks, I'm fine. I had breakfast before I came out.' He pulled a small notepad from his pocket and slid a pencil from between the pages. 'So, Lila, could you give me some idea of what you want done?' He wanted to seem professional, to deliver a quality business approach that would have customers returning to him time and time again.

'Certainly.' She was perched on the edge of the sofa, her back straight, her hands folded in her lap. In a navy and white striped top and jeans, she was dressed casually, but the way she was sitting hinted at discomfort or formality. Was she nervous? Anxious? Did she regret texting him?

He shook himself. This was ridiculous. He had come here to assess a job, nothing more, nothing less. And that was what he was going to do.

Lila ran through what she wanted done then took Ethan around the cottage to show him. He made plenty of notes on his pad and asked Lila lots of questions to ensure that he would provide the service she was looking for. The only place he really felt at all awkward was in her bedroom, a spacious room with a view over the back garden and fields beyond, with a double bed with plump pillows and a cornflower blue chenille throw, and what seemed to be antique furniture. There didn't seem to be any signs of a man anywhere, as if she had wiped all traces of her former fiancé from her home. Lila was lovely. She was pretty, softly spoken, friendly and she had an air of kindness about her that made him think that she would be a good friend to have.

Back downstairs, he tucked his notepad back in his pocket and followed Lila to the front door.

'I can definitely do the work.' He smiled. 'I'll put a quote together for you and email it over after the weekend if that's okay? I need to price some things up like paint, wood, sealer and a few other things.'

'Of course.' Lila smiled and something inside Ethan fluttered, making him press a hand to his belly. She was beautiful and when she smiled, her eyes lit up.

'Brilliant. Speak soon.'

Ethan opened the door and let himself out, wishing he didn't have to leave but knowing that he needed to take a walk and get some fresh air in order to think about how he was feeling right now. It was strange, unfamiliar, and he didn't know if it was excitement at the thought of his first job in charge of his own business or something else.

As he strolled away, enjoying the cool morning breeze on his skin he even mused that it could well be a combination of the two things.

6

Lila lay back on her yoga mat and closed her eyes. She let her breaths flow through her, their natural rhythm was her main focus, from the start of each inhale to the end of each exhale.

'Psst! Lila.'

She opened her eyes and turned to her right. Joanne was on the next mat, facing Lila, her face scrunched up.

'What?' She resisted the urge to tell Joanne off; they were meant to be focused on their breathing.

'I was thinking… you could go for a different colour for the hallway. Perhaps lavender or rose rather than white.'

Lila bit the inside of her cheek. Talking about paint during her Saturday morning yoga session at the village hall was the last thing she wanted to do. There were several sessions on a Saturday morning and she usually went to the earlier one as it was quieter but today she'd come to the later one with Joanne, something she was beginning to regret. She'd also seen a few familiar faces of people from the village who didn't go to the earlier sessions, and one of those was Freda Morris. She couldn't help wondering what Freda thought of Ethan's new business and if she was glad to have him back in Wisteria Hollow. In fact, everything seemed to be interrupting her relaxation this morning, especially thoughts about Ethan and his handsome face, warm smile and broad shoulders.

'Perhaps,' she replied, trying to shake all such images from her mind, then turned her head back to centre and closed her eyes again. She inhaled, slow and deep and exhaled, feeling her chest deflate.

'Or... duck-egg blue!' Joanne snapped into her thoughts again.

'Shhh!' Someone behind them was becoming irritated and Lila winced. She loved Joanne to bits but her concentration during yoga wasn't great and she tended to disturb those around her.

'Let's talk about it over coffee later,' Lila whispered, hoping that would silence her friend.

'Okay, cool.'

Lila straightened her spine, let her jaw and tongue relax and ran a body scan to check for any tension. As she focused on releasing the tension in her spine, a familiar smell brought her back to the room. She opened one eye, glanced sideways at Joanne and had to grit her teeth because Joanne was lying on her side peeling a banana.

'You're not supposed to eat during class,' Lila hissed.

'I'm starving. I slept in and didn't have time for breakfast.'

As she tried to contain her laughter, Lila's chest shook. Joanne was a lovely person but she really didn't care what people thought about her. How she'd managed to keep her job at the café, Lila had no idea, because Joanne was happy to call a spade a spade and never assumed airs and graces for anyone. Lila wished she could be more like Joanne sometimes, but she was always too aware of other people's thoughts and feelings. It was one of the reasons why she'd stayed with Ben for so long, she guessed. She'd always tended to put him first and to excuse his thoughtless behaviour, his forgetfulness (about birthdays, anniversaries and arrangements – unless they suited him) and his general selfishness that she'd so often put down to him being a man. Which was really quite sexist of her. At the end of the day, he was a human being and whatever someone's gender; it didn't excuse poor behaviour. But Lila had loved him and wanted him to be happy, often to her own detriment.

'Now bring your attention back to the room. Wriggle your fingers and toes. And when you're ready, open your eyes.' Finlay Bridgewater's soothing voice brought Lila back to the room and she sat up slowly and looked around. At the front of the hall, Finlay was in full lotus position, his back straight and hands pressed together against his muscular chest. He was a lovely young man and his yoga and mindfulness classes were very popular in the village.

As people sat up then got to their feet, the gentle hum of chatter filled the hall. Some people went up to the front to thank Finlay, some to admire him and some to find out more about other classes he offered. Lila knew that he also worked as a personal trainer and seemed to have a steady stream of local clients, a lot of them women with disposable income and spare time on their hands, like Roxie.

'That was good.' Joanne rolled up her yoga mat and tucked it under her arm.

'Did you actually do any of it?' Lila giggled. 'I saw you filing your nails, eating a banana and I'm sure that at one point you were snoring.'

'Lila, I was not!' Joanne scowled in mock anger. 'I was merely resting my eyes in pigeon pose. It's just that I have a bit of a stuffy nose.'

'I feel good now anyway.' Lila stretched her arms above her head, enjoying how loose her back felt. 'It's released all that tension in my neck and shoulders.'

'Lila.' Finlay approached them, his dark eyes warm, his dark brown beard perfectly fashioned on his square jaw. 'You did well today.'

'Thank you.'

'Your lung capacity is really developing.'

He smiled and she smiled back. He really was good-looking if a bit too physically perfect.

'What about me?' Joanne asked, causing Finlay to turn to her.

'Uhhh… yes, Joanne. You did well too. Good effort.'

Joanne grinned, her dimples appearing in her rosy cheeks, her green eyes bright and filled with mischief.

'I just think I could do with some help with my doggy down.'

'Sorry?' Finlay frowned. 'Doggy down?'

'Yes, you know.' Joanne put her mat down then bent over,

putting her hands on the floor in front of her with her behind in the air. 'I can't quite get this pose right.'

Finlay stared at Joanne then turned to Lila and she shrugged. Joanne hadn't got the pose quite right but Lila had a suspicion that Joanne was doing this deliberately.

'I'm sure I saw you doing it right earlier.' Finlay's voice had risen in pitch, now laced with what could be panic.

'Come help me!' Joanne's face was turning red with the strain of holding herself in the position and Finlay seemed to realise that he wasn't getting out of this easily. He sighed then went to Joanne and eased her hips up slightly, then helped her to spread her hands out further before placing a hand on her back to straighten it.

'There. Perfect, Joanne.'

Suddenly, there was a loud ripping noise that seemed to bounce off the walls and Finlay jumped back, catching his foot on Joanne's rolled up yoga mat and staggering backwards. He managed to right himself before he landed on the wooden floor.

'Joanne!' Lila helped her friend to stand up, wincing at the terrible smell. 'You didn't just fart in our yoga instructor's face did you?'

Joanne was red-faced and sweaty, but it could have been from the yoga pose or because she was embarrassed. Around them people were whispering and laughing but Joanne pushed her shoulders back and shrugged.

'My apologies, Finlay. That was… an accident.'

Finlay shook his head, his lips curving upwards into a smile.

'It's fine, Joanne. It's not the first time that's happened and I doubt it will be the last.'

As Finlay wandered away, saying goodbye to members of the class, Joanne tucked her mat under her arm and slid her feet into her trainers.

'Well, no one can accuse me of being fake with anyone can they?'

'They certainly can't.'

'Are you sure he's not into women?' Joanne eyed Finlay as they made their way to the door. 'I just keep thinking I'm picking up signals from him.'

'I don't know for certain, Joanne, but Roxie did say that he told her about a date he went on and that the person was called Sam. He wasn't specific so he could be straight or gay. Or perhaps he's bisexual or pansexual.'

'Food for thought.' Joanne licked her lips. 'Right... Come to the café with me and we can have some breakfast before I start my shift. My treat.'

'There's no need for you to treat me, Joanne. You're meant to be saving.'

'Yes but I get a generous staff discount. So it's on me.'

'Okay then.' Lila laughed. 'You get breakfast but next time it's on me.'

'Deal.'

They linked arms as they walked down the stone steps from the village hall, blinking in the brightness of the March morning. It looked like it was going to be a beautiful day.

'You're wasting your time there, Joanne.' Roxie shook her head.

'Yes, but am I? Am I really?' Joanne asked before taking another bite of toast.

Lila was enjoying a post yoga breakfast in the café with her friends. Lila and Joanne had bumped into Roxie as she walked her dog Glenda, and invited her to join them. The small fawn pug was now sitting on Roxie's lap being spoiled with pieces of toast dipped in runny egg.

'You are. I'm telling you that Finlay is not interested in women. At all.'

'How can you be sure?' Joanne raised her eyebrows.

'He told me about a date he went on with someone called Sam. I'm pretty certain Sam was a man.'

'But not fully certain?' Joanne asked.

'Well… no. But…'

'I think he finds me attractive. There's something in the way he looks at me.' Joanne took a swig of tea the wiped her mouth with a napkin.

'Not that you're not gorgeous, Joanne, because you absolutely are…' Roxie placed a hand on Joanne's arm. 'But perhaps he just looks at you like that because he's a very nice man. He does have such lovely brown eyes and they do appear to be quite intense.'

Joanne nodded, a smile playing on her lips. 'He has beautiful eyes.'

'But the intensity could be because he's short-sighted,' Roxie suggested.

Joanne giggled and Roxie joined in. Lila loved how her friends laughed at themselves and teased one another. Life wasn't easy for any of them; Roxie had concerns about her marriage and Joanne had been single for as long as Lila had known her. She'd had opportunities to date but usually found a way to sabotage them. It was why Lila suspected that Joanne might be making more of her attraction to Finlay than she actually felt; what better way to avoid getting into anything serious than paying attention to a gay man? Or a man who just wasn't attracted to her. Mutual attraction was important in any relationship.

She tried to ignore the rolling in her stomach as she thought of how Ben had made her feel so unattractive. If she'd been more beautiful, more vivacious, more interesting, known more about football and the offside rule and all those things that Ben liked, he might not have gone looking elsewhere.

'Lila!' Roxie snapped her fingers in front of Lila's face. 'Stop it.'

'Stop what?' Lila folded her arms over her chest, feeling suddenly cold in her yoga gear despite her hooded top.

'Thinking about *you know who*.'

'I wasn't.'

Roxie's eyebrows crawled up her forehead and her eyes widened. It was a look that could have got a government spy to spill his secrets.

'Okay... I was thinking about B... *you know who*... but not in a sad way. Well, not really. I was just thinking how lucky I am not to have to be with a man who doesn't think I'm wonderful anymore.'

'And you are wonderful, darling.' Roxie reached over and squeezed her hand. 'You deserve the very best in a partner and to be loved, respected and treasured. As does Joanne.'

'As do you, Rox.' Lila smiled. 'As do you.'

Roxie blinked then cleared her throat and shook her glossy dark hair.

'Yes, well. Yes. Indeed.'

Roxie leant forwards and kissed Glenda's wrinkled brow before offering her another piece of toast.

'Is Fletcher home today?' Lila asked, hoping he had made plans with his wife.

Roxie met Lila's eyes. 'He has a lunch meeting at the golf club with a client but he said he'll be home for dinner. So… let's hope, right?'

'I really do hope so.' Lila nodded. 'If not, you and Glenda are very welcome at mine.'

'I know, Lila. Thank you.'

'Here's to friendship.' Joanne raised her mug of tea and Lila and Roxie joined in. 'Now, I'd better get to work or I'll have to look for another job.'

Joanne got up and cleared the table but Lila and Roxie stayed where they were, not quite ready to leave just yet. The café was warm and cosy and their table in the window had a lovely view of the village green. And as Roxie started telling Lila about a story she'd heard on the radio that morning, Lila allowed herself to relax. Her life had changed in many ways over the past year, but the more she thought about it, the more she could see that it was for the better. Things with Ben hadn't been right for a long while. It had taken time and space for her to see that clearly, but now she could, and with every day that passed, she felt a bit more positive about the future.

She was taking it one step, one day at a time, flanked by the best friends a woman could have.

~

*E*than entered the café and quickly closed the door behind him, not wanting to let the cold air from outside in. It was a bright but chilly morning and his run had seemed like a good idea when he'd woken to sunshine streaming through his window, but when he'd actually gone outside, he'd wondered at the sense in it. However, run over, he was glad he'd gone – as he always was – and now he was going to treat himself, and his mother, to a pastry and a coffee. His mother had headed off to yoga this morning and would probably be peckish too.

He went to the counter and stood in the queue, peering up at the menu. Delicious aromas teased him, sweet and savoury, the uplifting smell of freshly ground coffee and baking bread. The cafe offered everything from sausage rolls to bacon and brie filled croissants, chocolate chip muffins and fluffy maple syrup pancakes to boiled or poached eggs, although how he'd transport the latter home and keep them runny, he wasn't sure.

Standing there, he listened to the murmur of voices, customers and staff, the frothing of the coffee machine and to the low hum of the refrigerators. Above all other noises was the voice of the radio DJ that was followed by some nineties R&B. The song took Ethan back to his youth and made him smile as he remembered easier times, less complicated times when life had seemed to promise future fulfilment and possibilities. He wondered if any adult ever felt that same sense of enduring hope that they sometimes felt as a child. Did life wring it out of everyone, or did some people escape unscathed? It seemed unlikely, as so many things could go wrong and if you loved anyone, there was always a risk that you'd suffer the pain of losing them, whether relative, lover or friend. But to live a life without love… that would be such a waste.

Laughter broke through his reverie and he looked across the café to the table by the window. He'd been so engrossed in his thoughts about what he'd fill his belly with that he hadn't noticed the women at the table by the window. As he watched, the one with long red hair got up and carried plates over to the counter. She set the plates down then pulled her wavy hair into a ponytail that she flipped around and fixed into a bun at her nape then she took the plates past the counter and through to the kitchen. The other two women stayed at the table and Ethan recognised them as Lila and Roxie. They were deep in conversation and Roxie appeared to have a small animal on her lap that she kept kissing. Lila looked incredible in workout gear with rosy cheeks that could have been caused by exercise, the warmth of the café or a hot drink she'd just consumed. It made him want to ask if she'd been running too or if she'd been to an exercise class this morning. The sunlight caught her hair through the window and made it shimmer like gold.

Ethan's breath caught in his throat as she seemed to sense his eyes on her and looked up. She smiled and waved at him and he waved back, his own cheeks flushing as he realised that she must have known he was staring at her. What an idiot he must seem. He could go over and make up some excuse or he could stay here, get some breakfast then leg it out of the café and act nonchalantly as he passed her. But before he had a chance to decide, Lila and Roxie stood up, donned coats and Lila picked up a yoga mat from under the table.

Ethan's heart sank as he watched Roxie, dog tucked safely in a large bag with just its head poking out, open the door. Lila held it open as Roxie left then went through herself, but before she closed it behind her, she met Ethan's eyes again and smiled. It was a big smile, a kind and pretty smile, and it warmed Ethan right through. Then she was gone, disappearing into the March morning.

As he ordered two bacon and egg rolls and two coffees, he tried to tell himself that the impact of the smile upon him had been so great because it showed kindness, and kindness couldn't be underestimated, but a voice at the back of his mind kept whispering that it was, in fact, because Ethan liked Lila and had wanted her to smile at him, so he had some hope that she might like him too.

~

'What are you smiling about?' Roxie asked as she and Lila walked away from the café and towards the village green. When they got there, Roxie placed her bag on a bench, got Glenda out and clipped her lead to her collar then set the dog down on the grass.

'Oh... just things.'

Lila watched as Glenda roamed around, head down, flat nose pressed to the grass as she sniffed hard. Life was so much simpler for dogs like Glenda, all she wanted was a warm bed, good food and a daily walk or two. She didn't care about marriage or relationships; she adored her human companions and trusted them implicitly. It must be wonderful to be able to have such complete faith in someone, to be free of the burdens of anxiety and insecurity that could plague human beings. Of course, Lila knew that dogs could have complicated personalities too, she wasn't oversimplifying things, but Glenda, as an example, seemed so content.

Lucky Glenda.

'Things? Things like… a handsome young man who we just saw at the café?' Roxie nudged Lila. 'The more I see of Ethan Morris, the more he grows on me. He's quite a dish.'

Lila shrugged, not wanting to admit that she had noticed how muscular Ethan's legs were in his running shorts, how broad his shoulders were and how his face glowed as he'd entered the café. He really was easy on the eye.

'He's okay, I guess. But my interest in him is strictly professional.'

'Of course it is, darling.' Roxie giggled. 'And soon you'll be able to watch him up a ladder in your bedroom in as professional a capacity as you like.'

'Roxie! He hasn't emailed me the quote yet so I don't even know for sure that he will be doing the work. If not I'll have to find someone else.'

'His quote will be reasonable, I don't doubt it. I saw the way he was looking at you just then and that man likes you too.'

'What do you mean *too*?' Lila grimaced, hoping her face was hiding how flattered she felt. Roxie thought Ethan liked her. What if that was true?

She shook herself. It really didn't matter because whatever Ethan's thoughts and feelings about Lila were, she did not have any for him. There would be no ogling the painter and decorator at all!

'I bet he's good with his hands.' Roxie pulled a small plastic bag out of her pocket and scooped up Glenda's deposit from the grass. 'Goodness, Glenda, we must keep you off the eggs.'

The dog peered up at Roxie, her pink tongue dangling from her mouth, her black eyes bright and shiny.

'The only reason I care about whether he's good with his hands is if he's good at painting, Roxie. Now please cut it out.'

'Oh love, I'm just teasing you.'

Roxie slid her free arm around Lila's shoulders and hugged her. The poo bag dangled precariously close to them and Lila held her nose. 'Roxie get rid of that, it stinks!'

'It does, doesn't it?'

Poo bag dropped into poo bin, Roxie pulled a small clear bottle from her bag and squirted hand sanitiser on her palm then rubbed it over both hands.

'Right, I'd better head home and find out if Fletcher plans on spending any time with us this weekend. What are you up to this afternoon?'

They were walking in the direction of Sunflower Street with Glenda plodding on ahead, her curly tail held high, her flexible lead allowing Roxie to pull her closer or give her more freedom.

'I have a hot date with a bubble bath and a book, then I'm going to get on with another crochet greyhound while I watch some Saturday evening reality TV.'

'Sounds relaxing.'

'It will be. That's one of the good things about being single; I don't have to sit through football matches or zombie movies that I'd prefer not to watch. Ben loved football and I spent so many Saturdays enduring it on TV and cheering him on from the sidelines as he played with his work team.'

'And now someone else is having to watch it with him and freeze on the sidelines as she watches him run around.'

'I hope for her sake that she likes football. I know lots of women do. But as for me, I just can't get into it.'

'Cricket is okay, tennis too and I love rugby, but football has no allure for me either.' Roxie shortened Glenda's lead as they slowed down then stopped outside Lila's cottage.

'You know where I am if you need me, Lila.'

'I do.'

They hugged then Lila opened her front door and Roxie walked away. Lila entered her hallway and closed the door behind her, enjoying the familiar scents of home and doing her very best to be positive about her freedom.

7
---

*E*than had emailed his quote to Lila and she'd replied asking when he could start. He was delighted to have secured his first job and, when he allowed himself to admit it, delighted by the thought of spending more time with her. They'd agreed that he could start the following Monday and now that day had arrived. It was a beautiful morning and as Ethan carried some of his equipment over to Lila's cottage, he breathed deeply of the sweet morning air. March had brought spring to Sunflower Street and it was glorious with pink buds on trees, daffodils, snowdrops and tulips creating rainbows of colour in borders and pots, and birds singing happily in the trees. Everything looked so much better in the sunshine and it lifted Ethan's spirits too.

He had bought a small white van to transport his equipment around but seeing as how Lila lived on the same street, he didn't need to drive to get there. It was strange knowing that she was just a few doors away, and he found himself looking for her every time he left his mother's house. He'd seen her several times and they'd waved, but apart from that, they were still basically strangers. He hoped he'd have the chance to get to know her a bit better while he worked at her cottage, although that thought also brought with it a certain amount of guilt.

Getting to know another woman wasn't a simple process. It was something he hadn't thought he'd ever want and it felt as though he was betraying Tilly, even though he was fairly certain he didn't want anything from Lila other than friendship. Tilly was, and always would be, in his heart and mind, but he found it so hard to let go of her and to fully accept that she wasn't coming back.

Outside Lila's cottage, he rested his ladder against the front wall and knocked on the door. It swung open almost immediately, as if Lila had been waiting for him in the hallway, and she smiled up at him.

'Good morning.'

'Morning, Lila.'

In faded jeans, fluffy slipper boots and a white shirt with her hair pulled into a short ponytail and her face free of makeup, she was breathtaking. Some women could pull this effortless look off so well and Lila did it with gusto. He realised he was staring when her cheeks flushed and she stepped back into the hallway.

'Come in. Where are you planning on staring… I mean *starting*?'

'I thought I'd work from the top down if that's all right with you?' he said, trying to pretend he hadn't noticed that she'd mentioned his staring.

How embarrassing!

'Of course. Would you like a cup of tea or coffee?'

'I'd love a tea please, milk, no sugar.'

'Go on up and I'll make the tea.'

Ethan nodded then started carrying things up the narrow staircase, taking care not to scratch the walls with the side of the ladder or the painting tray. When everything was in Lila's bedroom, he shook out the old sheets he'd brought to cover Lila's bed and furniture then moved everything to the centre of the bedroom, trying not to notice that the room smelt of her sweet fragrance, a heady mix of what he thought might be vanilla and jasmine. He was also trying not to think about that fact that just hours ago, Lila would have been lying in the bed, her pretty face relaxed in sleep, her limbs stretched out, her eyelashes fluttering on her smooth skin.

He took a deep breath and shook his head. He needed to get a grip and fast. Ethan was here to do a job and to start building his reputation as a good worker, not to fall for the clients.

Not that he was in the right place to fall for anyone, of course.

Not at all…

~

Lila sang to herself as she made a pot of tea then poured milk into two mugs. It was strange knowing that someone else was in her home, upstairs while she was downstairs. But also quite pleasant. She spent so much time alone now with just the cats for company, that having another human being around was comforting and something she could enjoy over the next few weeks while Ethan worked on her cottage.

Tea made, she picked up one mug and carried it upstairs to her bedroom. Ethan had already covered everything with sheets and her room smelt of an unfamiliar fabric softener.

'They're old sheets from my mother's,' he explained as she handed him the mug of tea.

'She didn't mind you using them?'

'Not at all. Said I was doing her a favour as she needs to have a good clear out.'

'I did that recently and it's very cathartic.' Lila smiled, trying not to stare at him but finding her eyes drawn to his dark hair and brown eyes, to the small mole on his left ear lobe that Lila had a sudden urge to touch. She tucked her hands into her jean pockets to stop herself acting on the impulse.

'That was why you were at the charity shop?'

'Yes. Getting rid of some things that were no longer of any use to me but that might be useful to someone else.'

'I remember something about a wedding dress?'

Lila stiffened. So he knew about Ben.

'Yes. I needed to get rid of it. And it helps raise money for the rescue greyhounds.'

'Even better.' He nodded.

'I don't know your mother very well, even though I've been here for about five years. Obviously, I know her but only to say hello to her.'

'She has kept herself to herself a bit more recently.'

'She's not the only one.'

Lila hung her head, wishing she hadn't said that.

'You too huh?'

She sighed. 'Only since… my uh… my…' What did she call him? *Ex? Ex fiancé? Ex boyfriend? Shithead?* 'My ex left.'

'Acrimonious, I take it?'

She nodded. 'Kind of. Very unpleasant actually. He uh… I mean, you probably know, but he jilted me at the altar. It was awful.' Heat crawled up her neck and into her cheeks as it always did whenever she told someone about what Ben had done. It was as if her body recalled the humiliation as well as her mind.

'He's a fool.'

Lila met Ethan's eyes and found kindness there. He wasn't judging, just offering support.

'Thank you.'

'So you've been lying low, have you?'

Lila nodded. 'It's been a strange year.' She pulled her hands from her pockets and folded her arms across her chest. 'But I'm coming out the other side.'

'I'm glad to hear it.' Ethan sipped his tea. 'Thanks for this. It's just how I like it.'

'You're welcome. Shout when you'd like another one.'

'Will do. And thank you.'

Lila turned to leave the room.

'Oh, Lila?'

'Yes?'

'I've left a bag in the hallway with my sandwiches in it. I just wanted to check that's okay? I could go home for lunch but I wasn't sure what time I'd be done with the first coat and it seemed easier to bring food with me.'

'No problem at all. Do you want me to put them in the fridge?'

'No need. They should be fine.'

'Okay then.'

Lila left the bedroom and padded down the stairs. Ethan seemed like such a kind, thoughtful man but she shouldn't get carried away. Ben had seemed like a good man in the early days of their courtship and look how that had turned out.

∼

*E*than stood back and surveyed the bedroom ceiling and the walls. They looked good, much fresher already with just one coat. He'd taken care with the painting, trying to ensure that there was an even coverage. The last thing he wanted was for his first customer to have to lie in bed staring at patchy painting.

The window that overlooked the back garden and fields beyond was open and sweet spring air filled the room. The scents of Sunflower Street in spring were familiar and his heart squeezed, taking him back to days when he'd played foxes and hounds in those fields, when he'd roamed the lanes with his friends picking fat, juicy blackberries that turned his lips and tongue purple in the late summer and early autumn, and of winters when it had snowed heavily and he'd run through the fresh snow leaving his mark then fallen backwards and made snow angels, sometimes with his mother when she'd been in a playful mood. He'd had a good childhood, even without a father around, and he had his mother to thank for that. She was a strong woman, admirable in her determination to keep things running smoothly, in the way she loved her son and built a stable life for him.

He'd noticed since he'd been home that she had good days and bad days; on the good days she was happy and busy, on the bad days she was tired and struggled to complete basic tasks like washing-up or pegging out the washing. He was trying to be as helpful as he could, to repay her for everything she'd done for him. He just hoped that she was going to be okay and that this was a temporary setback. She was all he had now and the thought of losing her was unbearable.

He went to the window and closed his eyes, letting the air wash over him, cleanse his mind and soothe the sad thoughts. Everything would be okay, it had to be. Worrying wouldn't change anything and neither would negative thinking of any kind.

He checked his mobile and was surprised to see that it was after eleven. He wanted to get another coat of paint on the bedroom before he took a lunch break, so he'd get that done then have his sandwiches. Lila had been very kind keeping him supplied with mugs of tea and had brought him some delicious homemade chocolate chip cookies at one point, so he wasn't ravenous, but he knew that in an hour or so he'd want something more substantial.

∼

Lila looked up from her crochet project and listened carefully. She could hear the murmur of a DJ on the radio upstairs and the occasional creaking of floorboards as Ethan moved around. There was something so reassuring about having another person in the cottage and she allowed herself to imagine for a moment that she wasn't alone, that she had someone there with her and in her life who cared. Dangerous territory probably, but it was nice to indulge herself for a few moments, to pretend that she had a man who loved her and would be there for her, no matter what. Over the years, she'd done the same when wishing she had supportive and loving parents. To have a mum and dad around who cared about her would have made her life a bit easier, she felt sure. The knowledge that there were two people in her corner, the two people who'd created her would have helped her to feel more secure and less lonely, surely? Sadly, it wasn't the case at all, and she had only herself and her friends, but then that was more than a lot of people had. Lila tried to be positive and grateful for what she had, to appreciate her lovely home and two cute cats, but on occasion she did wish for parents who gave a damn and for a partner to love.

She put the dog's head that she was crocheting down on the coffee table and stood up. There was definitely a funny noise coming from the hallway but she couldn't quite figure out what it was.

Lila crept towards the doorway, peered into the hallway and gasped.

'William Shakespaw! You naughty boy.'

The cat peered up at her, his nose and whiskers covered in something white that she assumed was either butter or cheese.

'What have you done, Willy?'

He blinked, stuck his head back in the bag that Ethan had left there, pulled out a sandwich then turned and ran through the hallway and into the lounge.

Lila hurried over to the bag to survey the damage. Bloody Willy had opened the bag, chewed through the cling film covering the sandwiches and had a good old munch. Lila wasn't sure how many sandwiches Ethan had brought but now he only had half of one left and that had teeth marks in it. Lila fed her cats well, so Willy hadn't done it out of hunger, but out of greed and mischief. And he did love cheese, which Lila didn't indulge him with, so he'd clearly sniffed it out and taken advantage of the unguarded sandwiches.

She picked up the bag, wondering how to tell Ethan that his lunch was gone. Obviously, she could offer to make him some food by way of an apology. In fact, she had a few things in the fridge that she could throw together, and Ethan had been working hard all morning, so it was the least she could do.

Lila turned and went through to the kitchen, dropped the plastic bag in the bin then washed her hands. The cat flap in the back door was swinging, so she knew Willy had heard her coming and dashed outside to stop her confiscating his prize.

As she opened the fridge, a smile played on her lips then a giggle burst from her. 'Bloody naughty cat!'

And he was naughty, but he had also given her the perfect excuse to make Ethan some lunch and, hopefully, to get to know him better. So she wasn't mad at all. In fact, she was secretly rather pleased. Probably without even meaning to, Willy had brought her a gift, and that was some company for lunch.

'Oh!'

From the kitchen, Lila heard Ethan's exclamation in the hallway, so she quickly dried her hands then went through to find him.

'What's wrong?' she asked.

He was rubbing his head and his T-shirt had risen slightly, exposing an inch of flat stomach with a dusting of dark hair. She dragged her gaze up to his face, fighting the urge to look at his tight abs again. Ben hadn't had tight abs. In fact, he'd been quite soft in spite of the football he played, but then he also liked beer and crisps and enjoyed those in front of the many football matches he watched on TV.

'I could have sworn I put my bag down there. The one with my sandwiches in it.'

'You did, Ethan, and… I have an apology to make.'

Lila smiled, hoping he'd be okay with this.

'See… I have two cats and the one, called Willy, short for William Shakespaw, is a bit… of a rogue.'

'A rogue, eh?' Ethan raised his eyebrows, amusement in his dark eyes.

'Yes. I came out here and found him enjoying your sandwiches. He has a thing about cheese.'

Ethan was nodding and smiling. 'So I guess I don't have any lunch left then?'

'Not the lunch that you brought with you, no, but I would like to offer you an alternative.'

'You don't need to do that.' He shook his head. 'I can pop back to Mum's and grab something.'

'Please. I'd like to. I mean… as long as you're happy to eat here. With me.'

God, I sound desperate…

'Are you sure?' he asked.

'Yes!' She bit her lip. 'I mean… yes. Please. I have plenty of food here.'

'Well, okay then. That would be lovely.'

'Great.' Lila almost clapped her hands. 'Come through to the kitchen.'

'I'm a bit messy though.' Ethan looked down at his paint splattered jeans and T-shirt. 'I guess I need to get some overalls, like a boiler suit or something.'

'It would save your normal clothes,' Lila agreed.

'I'll get some at the weekend.'

Lila walked through to the kitchen and Ethan followed her. For some strange reason her heart was pounding and her hands were trembling. It was ridiculous that offering someone lunch should make her feel so nervous. It wasn't as if she'd done anything wrong, just that she didn't know what was acceptable in this situation. But Ethan was working on her cottage and she worked from home, so surely having lunch together was innocent enough?

In the kitchen she gestured at the table.

'Take a seat.'

'I'd hate to get paint on your chair.'

'Here.' She handed him an old towel.

'Thanks.'

'You're welcome.'

He spread the towel over one of the chairs and sat down.

'This looks and smells amazing, Lila.' He gazed at the spread on the table and Lila's heart fluttered. Not only was he polite, friendly, and sweet but he was also appreciative. She went to brush off the compliment but then remembered that she didn't need to do that. This wasn't Ben, this was a completely different man. Compliments were allowed to be given and received.

'I'm glad you think so.' She carried the big bowl of salad she'd prepared to the table and set it down next to the plate of cold turkey, the slices of cheese and onion pie and the blue cheese potato skins. 'Help yourself, please. You've had a busy morning.'

'Thank you. I will.'

They filled their plates then tucked in, and as they talked and laughed, Lila found that her shakes faded away and she soon felt very comfortable indeed.

*E*than climbed the stairs to Lila's bedroom, his belly full and his face aching from smiling. Having his sandwiches stolen by a cat had worked out very well indeed. He'd spent the last hour eating the delicious lunch that Lila had put together, drinking cups of Earl Grey tea and laughing.

Lila was not just pretty and sweet, she had a great sense of humour and liked a lot of the same things Ethan did, like reading, binge watching box sets on TV (from crime and thriller to comedy), taking long walks in the countryside and learning about other countries so she could plan to travel to them one day. Ethan was only four years older than Lila, so they had watched similar TV shows as children, seen a lot of the same movies at the cinema and knew random facts about lots of celebrities from their generation. Ethan suspected that had they known each other growing up, they'd have been good friends.

In her bedroom, he looked around and nodded his approval at how the paint had dried on the ceiling and the walls. He'd give them another coat then let them dry overnight before deciding if he needed to do one more. If not, he could gloss the skirting boards then move on to the next job in Lila's cottage.

As he got to work, using a roller for the larger sections, he thought about Tilly and wondered if she'd have liked Lila. He suspected that she would have done. Tilly was friendly and kind and she'd have liked Lila's easy sense of humour and self-deprecating manner.

Thinking of his wife made his heart race but this time it wasn't grief or pain, it was guilt, because he was here, living his life and Tilly was gone, never coming back. It felt wrong that he was getting on with his life while his wife's had been cut so short. The grief counsellor had told him that he'd experience this, that it was perfectly natural and that he would process it and it would pass, but even so, it was still difficult to encounter. Ethan had told the counsellor that he would have given his life in exchange for Tilly's if it had been possible. He loved his wife and he'd have done anything to save her, even sacrificed himself if he could have done. So he had to try to make peace with himself. He had loved Tilly and she had loved him. But he was still here with a life to live.

'It's looking wonderful.'

Lila's voice brought him back to the room and he turned to meet her eyes. Her hair was down around her face now and it shone in the afternoon light, contrasting with the gentle blush of her cheeks and the bright blue of her eyes. She was beautiful and being near her was gently changing something inside Ethan, shifting his perspective, even though he was well aware that it could come to nothing. Even if Lila had been interested in him, he wasn't ready to move on.

Not yet.

Not just yet anyhow.

'I'm glad you're pleased,' he said, scratching at a blob of paint on his forearm.

Lila came to his side and looked at his arm then took it gently in one hand while she ran the thumbnail of the other hand over the paint. The blob gave and she dropped it into a black bag on the floor.

Their eyes met and Ethan realised that she hadn't let go of his arm. Her cool fingers were still wrapped around his skin and she seemed to notice at that exact moment. Her pupils dilated and her lips parted. Ethan tensed, afraid of what could happen yet curious to know what was possible.

A meow from the doorway broke the spell and Lila released him then stepped away.

'Oh there you are, Willy.'

The cat entered the room, his tail held high, his eyes surveying the walls as if he'd come to perform an inspection.

'Stay away from the paint, Willy, or you'll need a bath and that wouldn't be any fun for you or for me.'

'Don't cats hate water?' Ethan asked.

'They certainly do. I had to bath him once because he'd rolled in something out in the fields. It smelt like a dead animal, so there was no way I could have him walking around the cottage like that, sitting on the furniture and sleeping on my bed. Ben was really mad, but I told him that Willy had only done what came naturally to him. To be honest, I think Willy did it to annoy Ben because he rubbed against Ben's suit jacket that was hanging over the back of a kitchen chair and even dry cleaning couldn't get the smell out.'

She laughed and Ethan started to smile, enjoying watching how her eyes lit up when she was amused and how little dimples appeared in her cheeks.

'Perhaps Willy saw through this Ben?' Ethan suggested.

She nodded, her eyes glazing over now, as if she'd spoken out of turn by mentioning him.

'Yes. Not exactly a poster boy for a loyal, loving partner either.' She frowned. 'Sorry. That makes me sound so bitter and resentful and I'm not. Well... maybe just a teeny bit.'

'I'm sorry that Ben hurt you, Lila.'

She winced and Ethan wanted to reach out and hug her, to comfort her and reassure her that not all men were cheating idiots. It filled him with irritation that someone could hurt this lovely woman, wound her by betraying her trust and not appreciating her love. Loyalty was very important to Ethan and he imagined that it was to Lila too.

'Yes... Ben hurt me, but that's in the past now. Anyway, I'd better let you get on.' She flashed him a brief smile but her eyes were loaded with sadness and Ethan wished there was something he could do take away her pain. 'Come on, Willy.'

The cat meowed then followed her out of the bedroom and down the stairs, leaving Ethan alone with his thoughts and a thousand questions that he doubted he would ever have the courage to ask.

8

The next two and a half weeks flew past and soon Ethan's time at Lila's was coming to an end. The final day of March had arrived, bringing with it slightly milder days. Sunflower Street was beautiful with spring flowers in full bloom in garden borders, pots and hanging baskets. The weather made Ethan want to sing and whistle as he walked to work but then the thought of finishing at Lila's made his chest contract.

Ethan and Lila had fallen into a very pleasant routine. Every day, he'd break for lunch around one and Lila would make them some food. He'd tried to insist on bringing sandwiches but Lila had refused to allow it, telling him that it was nice to have company for lunch. So, by way of a thank you and not wanting to take advantage of Lila's kindness, Ethan had brought something with him every day: a bar of chocolate, some daffodils from his mother's garden, a tub of ice cream, and today, because it was his final day there, he'd brought a basket of goodies. His stomach clenched as he thought about its contents and what Lila might think about them, but he couldn't leave without showing her that he did appreciate everything she had done for him and how working at her cottage had helped restore his confidence in his manual skills. How it had helped him believe in the restorative powers of friendship and that life could be good again, because he'd actually had moments over the recent weeks when he'd felt happy.

He knocked on her door and waited, even though she'd told him to let himself in every morning. For Ethan, it just didn't seem right to do that, so he knocked and waited.

When Lila came to the door, his heart jumped. Today she was wearing a long red skirt with tiny white flowers on it and a loose white jumper that fell off one shoulder. As he followed her into the hallway, he found his eyes drawn to her shoulder, to the smooth creamy skin and the way her hair brushed against it as she moved. He wondered how her hair would feel if it brushed against his cheek, if he wound his fingers in it as he kissed her pretty mouth.

'I can't believe you're almost done here, Ethan,' she said as he closed the door behind him.

'Me neither. But I'll do a good check around today and if there's anything you're not happy with or if you spot anything after today, give me a shout and I'll come right back and sort it out.'

'Thank you.' She smiled and pushed her hair back behind her ears, exposing tiny diamond studs. He didn't think he'd seen her wearing earrings before but they were pretty and brought out the sparkle in her eyes. 'It's a gorgeous day, isn't it?'

'Beautiful.' *Just like you.* The way the observation sprang into his head made him smile. 'I uh… like your earrings.'

'Oh… thank you.' Lila touched them absently. 'They're an anniversary gift.'

'It's an anniversary?'

She nodded. 'I bought them for myself to celebrate not getting married a year ago today.'

'So today's the day, eh?'

'It is and the earrings are to remind me what a lucky escape I had.'

'You did have a lucky escape. I hate to think that Ben hurt you but if you'd married him, he probably wouldn't have made you happy.'

'I don't think he would. Anyway, a year has come and gone and I'm moving on with my life. Hell, I even bought myself diamonds.'

'And why not?' Ethan grinned at her. 'I brought a picnic for lunch. I thought that if it stays warm enough we could eat outside? If you fancy it, that is.'

'Oh, wow!' She took the basket from him. 'How considerate of you.'

He shrugged. 'It's nothing fancy, just something to say thanks for making me so welcome.'

'Ethan, you've been doing work for me. I'm grateful to you and I have a feeling that your quote was very reasonable for the work you've done.' She smiled. 'I know I probably shouldn't say that, should I? But I can't pretend, it's not in my nature and you've done such a great job here. My cottage is like new and I'm so excited about enjoying the rest of spring and then summer here as well as the rest of the year. Everything feels so fresh and new.'

'I'm delighted to hear that.' He nodded at the basket. 'There are some things in there that should probably go in the fridge to keep them fresh. And… you know… to protect them from Willy.'

Lila giggled. 'Have you brought cheese?'

'And ham.'

'Then I had better get them in the fridge and pronto.'

'I'll just take a look around and check everything then add any finishing touches.'

'Great.'

Ethan watched as Lila headed through to the kitchen then he climbed the stairs, more than a little bit sad that this would probably be the last time he'd be inside Lila's home.

～

Lila set the picnic basket down on the kitchen table and realised that she was grinning. Having Ethan around had been so enjoyable and now he'd come on his final day with a basket filled with goodies. What a lovely way to celebrate her anniversary. It wasn't the way she'd envisaged her wedding anniversary being, but then she'd had no idea that Ben would do what he did. Therefore, she would be happy to celebrate not marrying Ben and even happier to enjoy lunch with Ethan, a man she was starting to believe in the more she got to know about him.

She lifted the lid of the basket and peered inside. There was a bottle of champagne, a block of cheddar and a wedge of creamy brie, a packet of thick deli ham and a tub of shiny black olives. She put everything in the fridge then returned to the basket and pulled out the small square box.

'Champagne truffles!' She gasped. 'He shouldn't have done this,' she said to Willy and Cleo. The cats were watching her from their vantage point in the sunlight that was pouring through the open back door. She returned the truffles to the basket then switched the kettle on.

Today they would enjoy a picnic lunch in her garden, sip some expensive looking fizz and this enjoyable time would come to an end. It brought a lump to Lila's throat to think that this was it, that Ethan would move on to work on someone else's house and Lila's cottage would be quiet once more. Having Ethan around had been very pleasant. Though he was quiet as he worked, he seemed to fill her home with life, to bring a gentle cheer along with him and she was going to miss knowing that he was near, that when he left in the evening, he would return the next day. But he was a workman, had been here to paint and decorate, to mend and improve her cottage. Lila couldn't forget that or let the fact that they had spent time together cloud the reality that for Ethan, this was probably no more than a professional relationship, and he was just a friendly man with a kind heart. Yes, they had talked about themselves and their lives but not discussed deeper issues, not got to know each other on a more emotional level, and it would have been strange if they had because he was there to work not to fall in love.

Fall in love?

Where had that come from?

Lila was not in love, not falling in love and not remotely interested in falling for someone. Not now and she didn't think she ever would be. She just liked Ethan, that was all. No more, no less. He was the first man she'd spent any time with since Ben had left and her thoughts were muddled, her heart was vulnerable. Ethan was a friend and she hoped with all her heart that he would continue to be her friend because the thought of him disappearing from her life completely was hard to digest.

~

*E*than sat back in the chair, leant his head against the wall behind him and closed his eyes. Perfect moments were hard to find but this was one of them. After he had finished up at Lila's, they had come out into her back garden to have lunch and it had been lovely.

The sun was shining, birds were singing, the air was fragrant with sweet flowers and herbs that grew in Lila's pots and borders and the conversation had flowed freely. He'd told Lila more about his childhood, his life in Tonbridge and she'd told him more about her background.

Lila hadn't had what could be described as a great childhood, having two parents who apparently didn't want her in the first place — they had told her she was an accident and that her arrival had hampered their lifestyle. As Lila had grown up, they had provided for her physically but not been there emotionally, and it was why Lila no longer had a relationship with them. What Lila told him about her parents made him even more grateful for his mum. People shouldn't have children if they didn't want them; it wasn't fair on the children to be born into such circumstances, he thought. However, in spite of this, Lila had turned out strong and independent, kind and sweet.

'What are your plans now?' Lila asked, so he opened his eyes.

'Oh I don't know... stay here and take a nap.'

She smiled, bringing those adorable dimples to her cheeks.

'That sounds lovely and after the champagne, I could take a nap too, but I meant for the next few weeks and months.'

Ethan nodded. 'Well... I'm keen to make a go of my business, so I'll be focusing on growing my customer base. I also want to spend some time with Mum because the past few years have made it difficult for us to get much quality time. I mean... really, my head wasn't in anything important after... after Tilly passed away and now I feel I owe Mum some time and attention. Does that make sense?'

'Of course it does.' Lila inclined her head. 'I'm sure your mum understands why you've been—'

'Drifting?'

'Yes. If that's how you see it.'

Ethan ran his gaze over her flushed cheeks and golden hair, over her clear skin and pretty little nose. If only he was in a better place emotionally but the thought of not being strong enough for her or giving her the love and commitment she deserved would put a lot of pressure on him and he coulnd't bear to let her down.

'I do. I have been drifting, not committing to anything or anyone, not even my mum. *Unable* to commit is more accurate.'

'Oh, Ethan I'm sorry.'

He shook his head. 'It's certainly not your fault, but thank you.'

He had told Lila that he'd lost Tilly to cancer and she'd admitted that she knew some of the details, then she'd sat quietly, waiting for him to talk if he wanted to. And he found that a part of him did want to open up to her. However, he didn't want Lila to see him differently, as a widower and someone to pity instead of as a friend and as a man, and telling her all about Tilly might change how she saw him. He was surprised to find that he actually cared about her opinion of him and it was revelatory because he hadn't cared about how people saw him in a long time.

'What about your future?' she asked. 'Will you stay here or move on?'

He shrugged. Who knew what the future held?

'I'd like to stay here for a while, perhaps settle in Wisteria Hollow again. The village is lovely, the people are too and Surrey is a great place to be.'

'A good place to heal?'

'Hopefully.'

He held her gaze across the table and before he knew what he was doing, he reached out and squeezed her hand. Lila looked shocked initially but then she relaxed and caressed his hand with her thumb.

'I hope you can heal, Ethan. You deserve to be happy.'

'So do you, Lila. What are your plans?'

'I'm going to work hard to grow my business too. I neglected it after Ben left and neglected myself.'

'You should never be neglected, Lila, and Ben was a fool for leaving you, but we've already established that fact several times.' He smiled to show he was teasing her about the times he'd become annoyed with a man he'd never met.

'Perhaps, but if he wasn't happy then staying with me, marrying me would have been a big mistake. Imagine if we had got married and had children. It would have been awful to know he'd have felt trapped. Or, he might have left me and them, and that would have been so much worse. At least he went when he did, although I do think he could have done it a bit more carefully.'

'Idiot!' Ethan shook his head and Lila laughed.

'I love it when you call him that.'

'You were saying you're going to grow your business but what of your life apart from that?'

She pursed her lips and frowned.

'I thought I wanted to get married and have a family. After my childhood, I think I wanted to have a stable, loving family unit of my own. Any therapist would probably tell you that it's perfectly natural to yearn for that security, I guess. But that was before Ben left and now… I'm not sure.'

'I wanted a family too.' Ethan's chest tightened. 'It was something I took for granted… I assumed it would happen but none of us know what's around the corner, do we?'

'We don't.'

They sat in silence for a while and Ethan watched as Lila's cats stretched out in the spring sunshine, their furry bellies exposed to the gentle warmth. Ethan's mobile buzzed so he pulled it from his pocket and checked the screen. It was his mother asking him to pick up something for heartburn from the shop.

It was probably a sign that it was time for him to make a move.

'I'll give you a hand with the dishes then I'd better get going as Mum wants something for heartburn.'

He stood up and stretched then carried some of the plates inside and Lila followed him.

'Is she okay?' Lila asked.

'Her text just said she had heartburn so I guess so.'

'I have some indigestion tablets here that you can take.'

'There's no need. I can buy some.'

'Please, I insist.'

Lila opened a cupboard and brought out a basket then rooted around in it and produced a packet of tablets.

'What if you need them?' Ethan asked.

'I have more upstairs.'

'Okay, if you're sure.'

'I am.'

Lila put the basket away and turned to Ethan. 'Don't worry about the dishes. I'll pop them in the dishwasher when you're gone.'

'I don't like to eat and run.'

'You're not. We've been sitting in the garden for two and a half hours. And it's no problem. I might actually take that nap when you go anyway.'

'Right then… I've packed up all my equipment and will take most of it now but if it's okay, I'll come back for the ladder later?'

'Of course.'

They walked through the cottage to the front hallway and Ethan reached for the door handle.

'Ethan, wait!'

The urgency in Lila's voice surprised him and he froze. Lila placed a hand on his arm and he turned to her. What he saw in her eyes shocked him to his core because it was what he'd seen in his eyes in the mirror. It was a messy mixture of emotions from confusion, to hope, to anguish, to need, and more. Standing in front of him was a woman who wanted to live, who wanted to love and be loved, but who had been hurt and was terrified of being hurt again.

'What is it, Lila?' he asked as he gently stroked her cheek with his free hand, unable to stop himself touching her in this moment. 'Tell me.'

She frowned then rose onto her tiptoes and took his face in both of her hands. He lowered his head to hers and as their lips touched, a spark lit and electricity ran through his entire body making his heart race and his body awaken as if from a deep sleep. He wrapped his arms around her and held her close, kissing her softly at first then harder, feeling her mould into him as they gave in to their desire.

He was about to scoop her up in his arms and carry her upstairs when something inside him screeched like the brakes of a car. He broke off the kiss and shook his head.

What was he doing? How could he kiss another woman when he was still married to Tilly, still loved Tilly and always would do?

Lila gazed up at him, her face contorting with changing emotions, her eyes filled with fear and doubt. Ethan's throat burned and he wanted to speak to her, to reassure her, but he couldn't say a word.

'Ethan… I'm sorry. This was wrong, wasn't it? Too soon? Too much? Oh my god, I'm so embarrassed. I shouldn't have reached for you, shouldn't have kissed you. Please… forgive me. It was the champagne and the sunshine and it all went straight to my head and…' She pushed her hands back through her hair and held them there, Ethan could see that she was holding tight because her knuckles had turned white. He hated himself for doing this to her, just as he had feared he would.

Ethan sucked in a breath and released it, but still he couldn't speak.

'You should go, Ethan. Please. Go now.'

Lila lowered her hands and pointed at the door. Her beautiful eyes glistened with tears and Ethan wanted to pull her close and comfort her, but something inside him had snapped and he was unable to be what she needed him to be right then and there. He had a terrible sense of letting her down just as he had let Tilly down.

So he opened the door and stepped outside.

'Ethan?'

He turned, wanting her to reach for him again but she didn't, she was merely holding out his toolbox and painting tray.

'Goodbye, Ethan.'

Lila closed the door then, and as her lovely face disappeared from view, he gasped. This was painful, it was overwhelming and it was…

Like waking up after a long, long time asleep.

Because finally, something other than his grief for Tilly had made him feel deeply again and that something was Lila Edwards.

9

Lila ran her hand over Cleo's soft fur and the cat purred loudly. Thank goodness for her cats and friends, she didn't know how she'd have got through the last four weeks without them. After Ethan had left (following their picnic and *that* kiss) Lila had been devastated. She had thought there was a connection between them, had read more into his offering of the picnic than she should have and Ethan had fled her home without saying a word.

It had brought all of the pain and confusion surrounding Ben's abandonment of her right back and she'd had to face up to it, really face up to it and deal with it. Roxie had been her rock, hugging her, drying her tears, filling her wine glass then, finally, telling her that she had to get up and keep going, that she couldn't allow another man to bring her life to a halt.

But for Lila, it hadn't been Ethan who'd brought her life to a halt, it had been Ben and everything he'd stood for, everything Lila had believed they had. Obviously, Ethan's apparent rejection of her following such a passionate kiss had knocked her confidence, had been quite humiliating, but she didn't know him well enough to be deeply wounded by him. She liked Ethan, liked him a lot, but when he'd left her house that day, she'd been forced to take a good look at herself and accept that she wasn't ready to be with another man. Not yet, anyway. However, the kiss with Ethan and their time together had given her hope, because she had felt something for him. It had been something positive that had made her heart beat faster, awakened desire inside her and made her realise that she did have a lot to offer a relationship; she was not hideous, undesirable and worthless. Lila was a warm, strong, caring person and one day, she might well meet the man who would see that. Until then, she'd be just fine as she was, and if it never happened, then that would be all right too because she had her cats, her friends and her business to focus on. A loving romantic relationship would simply be the icing on her wonderful cake.

The weekend after Ethan had fled her cottage, she had sent him a text to apologise and three days later he had replied, as if he'd had to take the time to think about how to respond. He'd told her she had no need to say sorry then apologised for leaving as he had and asked if it was okay to pick up his ladder. He had come an hour later and Lila had opened the door, handed him the ladder and the picnic basket (that he seemed to have forgotten about) then they'd made stilted conversation. Ethan had looked awful. His skin had been pale, dark shadows sat under his eyes and she'd longed to invite him in for coffee and a chat but been afraid that he might think she wanted more.

So, instead, she'd wished him well and he'd left, hopefully to go back to bed for a few hours judging by how tired he'd seemed. Everyone had things to work through and Ethan seemed to be in that place right now. Lila knew from her own experience that the kindest thing she could do would be to give him space. If he wanted to speak to her, to be friends as he'd told her he did, then she'd be there when he felt ready to talk.

'Come on then, Cleo, let's strip the bed so I can get the sheets on the line to dry. It's a beautiful day and there's nothing better than line dried sheets, is there?'

Cleo meowed then jumped off Lila's lap and they made their way upstairs. Simple pleasures like fresh bed linen, hot cups of tea, and food with friends were things that Lila was learning to treasure. She had always appreciated them but as she healed from her breakup with Ben, she was seeing things as if through new eyes and she liked valuing the things that really mattered.

'Morning, Mum.'

Ethan carried the mug of tea to his mother's bedside table and set it down on a coaster. The room was dark and his mum had slept in much later than usual, so he'd come to wake her up because he knew she hated missing what she called 'the best part of the day'.

He opened the curtains and turned back to the bed, expecting to see his mother rubbing her eyes and yawning, but she was lying on the floor beside the bed and she was completely still.

The room was deathly quiet.

He held his breath and listened, strained to hear her exhale, shuffle or even emit a little snore.

Nothing.

'Mum!'

He rushed over to her and gasped. Her face was grey, her lips blue and her hands were pressed to her chest.

'Mum! Are you okay?'

He pulled his mobile from his pocket and dialled 999.

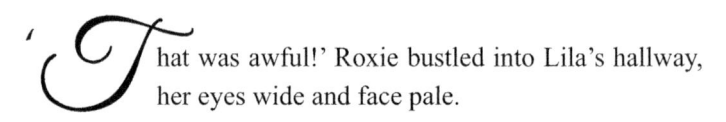

～

'That was awful!' Roxie bustled into Lila's hallway, her eyes wide and face pale.

'What was?' Lila took hold of Roxie's shoulders and rubbed them gently, hoping to reassure her friend.

'Didn't you hear the siren?'

'What siren?'

'Oh, Lila… An ambulance came hurtling through the village and stopped in front of Freda Morris's house. The paramedics went inside and when they emerged they had Freda on a stretcher.'

'What?' Lila's stomach dropped to her slippers. 'Is she okay?'

'I honestly don't know. She had an oxygen mask on and Ethan was at her side, poor man. He got in the ambulance with her and it sped away.'

Lila tried to process what Roxie was telling her. Ethan's mother had been taken to hospital. That was worrying, especially the fact that she'd been taken in an ambulance. She hoped with all her heart that Freda would be all right and that Ethan would too. Suddenly, the past few weeks of questioning his behaviour and her own, especially the kiss they'd shared seemed irrelevant. As far as Lila knew, Ethan had no one else and she wanted to be there for him.

'I have to go to the hospital.'

'What?' Roxie frowned at Lila. 'But why?'

'I can't leave him there alone. He has no one else.'

'Lila… he's not your responsibility.'

'I know that, Roxie, but he's a friend and… you'd help a friend in need wouldn't you? Hell, you'd help *anyone* in need.'

Roxie nodded. 'That's true. I hate the thought of anyone struggling alone.'

'Well I feel the same. Ethan might not be the man for me but he's definitely a friend, and even if he decides that he doesn't want that from me, I don't care. I just want to let him know that I'm here if he needs me.'

'Then go get him, girl!' Roxie smiled. 'He'll be glad to have you there, I'm sure.'

Lila grabbed her bag from the kitchen and her coat off the hook in the hallway. 'Will you feed the cats if I'm out all day?'

'Of course I will.'

'You have your key?'

'I do.'

'Good. I'll let you know what's happening.'

'Please do. And Lila?'

'Yes?' Lila was already opening the door and she swayed with impatience, keen to get to Ethan as quickly as possible.

'Please take care.'

'Of course I will.'

She stepped out into the street.

'Lila!'

'Yes?' She ground her teeth together.

'One more thing.'

'Yes, Roxie?'

'You might want to change your footwear.'

Lila glanced down at her feet. She was still wearing her hedgehog slippers and they wouldn't be great for driving in. Roxie was right; she had better put some shoes on.

~

*E*than paced the hallways of the cardiac intensive care unit. His mother had been rushed into surgery following their arrival at the hospital. The operation had been successful and the consultant surgeon had told him that his mum had a blocked coronary artery and it had caused angina. The pain had caused her to faint when she'd tried to get out of bed. They'd performed a coronary angioplasty to stretch open the artery then placed a stent there to allow the blood to flow more freely. Apparently, his mother could go on to make a full recovery, but she would need to watch her diet and to avoid stress where possible.

Ethan had been confused about why this had happened to his mother, because to his knowledge, she lived a healthy lifestyle, but the consultant surgeon had told him that it could happen to anyone, although certain factors could make it worse. In Freda's case, one of the main coronary arteries had become narrowed and hardened, which had led to angina. It was likely that it had been triggered by stress or physical activity. Ethan was devastated at the thought that his mother could have been so stressed that it affected her health, but the consultant reassured him that it was most likely an accumulation of factors. It could also be hereditary, so the consultant had advised Ethan to visit his GP for advice and possibly some tests.

'Ethan?'

He froze. He'd thought he was alone here, completely alone. He hated hospitals, found the clinical scents brought back so many awful memories of Tilly's cancer battle. The sounds of hushed voices and beeping machines, of soft-soled shoes and scrubs swishing as medical staff moved around the wards all gave him chills. He was battling to stay strong, to keep his head above water but it was so difficult and all he wanted was someone to lean on.

'Ethan?'

A hand touched his shoulder and he turned to find Lila standing there, her face etched with concern, her eyes glistening.

'Lila?' he whispered.

'I came as soon as I heard. Traffic was awful then it took me almost an hour to park, but I wanted to come. I know you don't really have anyone else. I can go if you want? I don't want to impose but I just…' Her eyes searched his face and he swallowed hard, afraid that he was about to crumple, but her hands found his and she led him to a chair. She sat next to him, still holding on to him as if holding him together.

'Is… is your mum okay?'

He nodded, not trusting himself to speak.

'Are you?' she asked.

A tear slipped from his eye and rolled down his cheek. Lila gently brushed it away with the pad of her thumb then slid her arm around his shoulders. He took some deep breaths, trying to steady himself but it was no good. He couldn't hold it in any longer, and when Lila pulled him into her arms and held him tight, he finally let go.

10

Three weeks had passed since Freda's operation and she'd been allowed to come home two days ago because she'd made a good recovery and because she had Ethan there to care for her. Since that day at the hospital, where Lila had gone to Ethan and he'd cried in her arms, they had continued to see each other daily. Ethan had initially been embarrassed about breaking down but Lila had reassured him, told him that it was a positive thing to show his emotions and he had thanked her for being there. The fact that he had exposed himself emotionally made Lila feel more relaxed around him, as if she knew him better than she had ever known Ben.

Today she was heading over to Freda's with some homemade soup for lunch and she was looking forward to spending the afternoon there while Ethan went to look at some work for a prospective client. The client was Roxie, and Lila was glad that her friend had decided to offer Ethan some work. After he'd finished at Lila's, and with his mother being rushed into hospital, he'd been unable to work, so he needed another job now to get things off the ground. He'd been worried about leaving his mother alone so Lila had offered to help out by checking in on Freda but without making it look as though she was checking in. Freda hated being what she called *a burden* and wanted her independence back as quickly as possible, so Ethan and Lila were trying to give her that while making sure she was taking it easy.

Lila knocked on Freda's door then smiled as Ethan opened it. His dark hair was messy and he had a few days' stubble dusting his jaw, but he was, in her opinion, gorgeous. His dark eyes appraised her and she was glad she'd made the effort to wear the blue shirt that he said brought out the colour of her eyes and that went so well with jeans.

'Good morning, Lila.'

He stepped backwards and she entered the hallway.

'Morning, Ethan.' Lila let him take the rucksack that contained her crochet kit and work in progress, a large blanket made up of different coloured granny squares. She'd made one and listed it on her website and it had sold within hours, then she'd had three more commissioned, so she was going to be busy for a while. 'How's your mum?'

He glanced behind him, put Lila's bag down then leant closer. 'She's good. She's looking forward to crocheting more squares apparently because it makes her feel useful.'

'Your mum is really good at granny squares and I'm grateful for her help.'

'I'm grateful for yours.'

He gently cupped her chin and ran the pad of his thumb over her lips then moved closer and tilted her chin. He held her gaze and she sank into the depths of his brown eyes. When their lips met, she melted into his arms and he kissed her slowly, his lips warm and soft, his one hand still holding her chin, the other hand finding its way to her nape and sliding up into her hair. Shivers of delight ran down her spine and she wrapped her arms around his neck and pulled him closer.

When they finally broke apart, Ethan kissed her cheeks, the tip of her nose and her forehead.

'I'm grateful for you, Ethan Morris and for every day that we spend together.'

They had talked at length after Lila had comforted him at the hospital and decided to take things slowly. They had agreed to get to know each other and to be sure about what they wanted before they moved their relationship to the next level, but with every kiss that they shared, Lila felt more certain that Ethan was a good man and that he'd never hurt her. Ethan had confessed that he was worried that he'd lose her, that she could get ill as Tilly had done and that was a fear he was gradually coming to terms with. Lila had admitted that she was nervous about being in another relationship and that it would take some time for her to be able to trust again.

There were no guarantees, there were no certainties, but as long as they maintained an open and honest dialogue and accepted that they should live for today, enjoy being together in the moment, then they were on the right path.

'Ethan… I know we're not supposed to look too far ahead and that we need to focus on the here and now, but I do have a feeling that this is going to be a good summer for us.'

He smiled and nodded. 'Me too, Lila. I'm starting to believe that as long as we have each other, we can cope with anything.'

He took her hand and led her through to the lounge where Freda was waiting. Just like the spring shoots on Sunflower Street had grown tall and strong, something was growing between Lila and Ethan. It was something good, something very positive and something worth nurturing.

Lila took a deep breath then as she exhaled, she let go of her remaining fears and reservations, and allowed her heart to fully surrender to the man she knew she was falling in love with.

The End

WANT MORE?

Now read ***Summer Days on Sunflower Street…***

AND…

Visit my website here - https://rachelgriffithsauthor.com to subscribe to my newsletter, to download free short stories and find out what's next.

Also, take a look at ***Also by Rachel Griffiths*** for plenty more delightfully uplifting stories!

DEAR READER,

Thank you so much for reading *Spring Shoots on Sunflower Street*. I hope you enjoyed the story.

I would be so grateful if you could leave a rating and a short review to share what you enjoyed about the story.

Visit my website here - https://rachelgriffithsauthor.com to subscribe to my newsletter, to download free short stories and find out what's next.

Take a look at *Also by Rachel Griffiths* for plenty more delightfully uplifting stories!

With love,
Rachel X

ABOUT THE AUTHOR

Rachel Griffiths is an author, wife, mother, Earl Grey tea drinker, gin enthusiast, dog walker and fan of the afternoon nap. She loves to read, write and spend time with her family.

WANT MORE?

Visit my website here - https://rachelgriffithsauthor.com to subscribe to my newsletter, to download free short stories and find out what's next.

Take a look at ***Also by Rachel Griffiths*** for plenty more delightfully uplifting stories!

ACKNOWLEDGMENTS

Thanks go to:

My gorgeous family. I love you so much! XXX

My author and blogger friends, for your support, advice and encouragement.

Everyone who buys, reads and reviews this book.

ALSO BY RACHEL GRIFFITHS

Cwtch Cove Series

Christmas at Cwtch Cove

Winter Wishes at Cwtch Cove

Mistletoe Kisses at Cwtch Cove

The Cottage at Cwtch Cove

The Café at Cwtch Cove

Cake And Confetti at Cwtch Cove

A New Arrival at Cwtch Cove

A Cwtch Cove Christmas (A collection of books 1-3)

The Cosy Cottage Café Series

Summer at The Cosy Cottage Café

Autumn at The Cosy Cottage Café

Winter at The Cosy Cottage Café

Spring at The Cosy Cottage Café

A Wedding at The Cosy Cottage Café

A Year at The Cosy Cottage Café (The Complete Series)

The Little Cornish Gift Shop Series

Christmas at The Little Cornish Gift Shop

Spring at The Little Cornish Gift Shop

Summer at The Little Cornish Gift Shop

The Little Cornish Gift Shop (The Complete Series)

Sunflower Street Series

Spring Shoots on Sunflower Street

Summer Days on Sunflower Street

Autumn Spice on Sunflower Street

Christmas Wishes on Sunflower Street

A Wedding on Sunflower Street

A New Baby on Sunflower Street

New Beginnings on Sunflower Street

Snowflakes and Christmas Cakes on Sunflower Street

The Cosy Cottage on Sunflower Street

Snowed in on Sunflower Street

Springtime Surprises on Sunflower Street

Autumn Dreams on Sunflower Street

A Christmas to Remember on Sunflower Street

Secret Santa on Sunflower Street

Starting Over on Sunflower Street

The Dog Sitter on Sunflower Street

Autumn Skies Over Sunflower Street

A Year on Sunflower Street (Sunflower Street Books 1-4)

Standalone Stories

Christmas at The Little Cottage by The Sea

The Wedding

The Cornish Garden Café Series

Spring at the Cornish Garden Café

Summer at the Cornish Garden Café

Autumn at the Cornish Garden Café

Winter at the Cornish Garden Café